# T.A.N.

*An Erotic Novella*

K.L. Hall

B. Love Publications

**T.A.N. (Toxic A*s N***a): An Erotic Novella**

# T.A.N. Synopsis

Jahtavian Nichols is a cancer.

The toxic, slow-growing kind you never see coming until it's too late.

He's a playboy with one goal: to seduce as many women as possible, *especially* if they are friends.

Ten years ago, he used me and threw me away.

He deceived me. Humiliated me. Made me swear off love.

Everyone else may have let it go, but I haven't forgotten… or forgiven him.

In fact, I'm going to make sure he never does anything like that again.

You see, I'm not the same delicate, shy wallflower he hit and forgot.

I was an easy target before. I couldn't see a red flag from a mile away.

I *will* get the revenge I've always craved. Because this time?

I won't be the one being used. I'll be the one taking what I want from him.

I've spent the last decade formulating my borderline-obsessed plan.

Sweet revenge is the name of the game now, and Jah is *my* prey.

I move in next door to him with two things in mind: seduce and scheme.

I won't fall victim to his bedroom eyes or get mystified by his charm.

I'll make him pay, even if it breaks me twice.

# Author Note

The inspiration behind Jah's character came from a Six Brown Chick's Weekly Twitter Chat, #SBCChat. A man wrote in and said his kink was meeting a woman with a tight-knit friends group and fucking them all one by one. It turned him on to see the women struggle to remain "friends" with his girlfriend after they've been sexed up by him. Once the woman is strung out and ready to choose him over her friends, he leaves and moves on to a new group of women to run through. If that's not a toxic person, I'm not sure what is. While the content of this story is fictional, in reality, we know there's a toxic nigga lurking around every corner. Be safe out there ladies, and enjoy this erotic revenge read with a HEA.

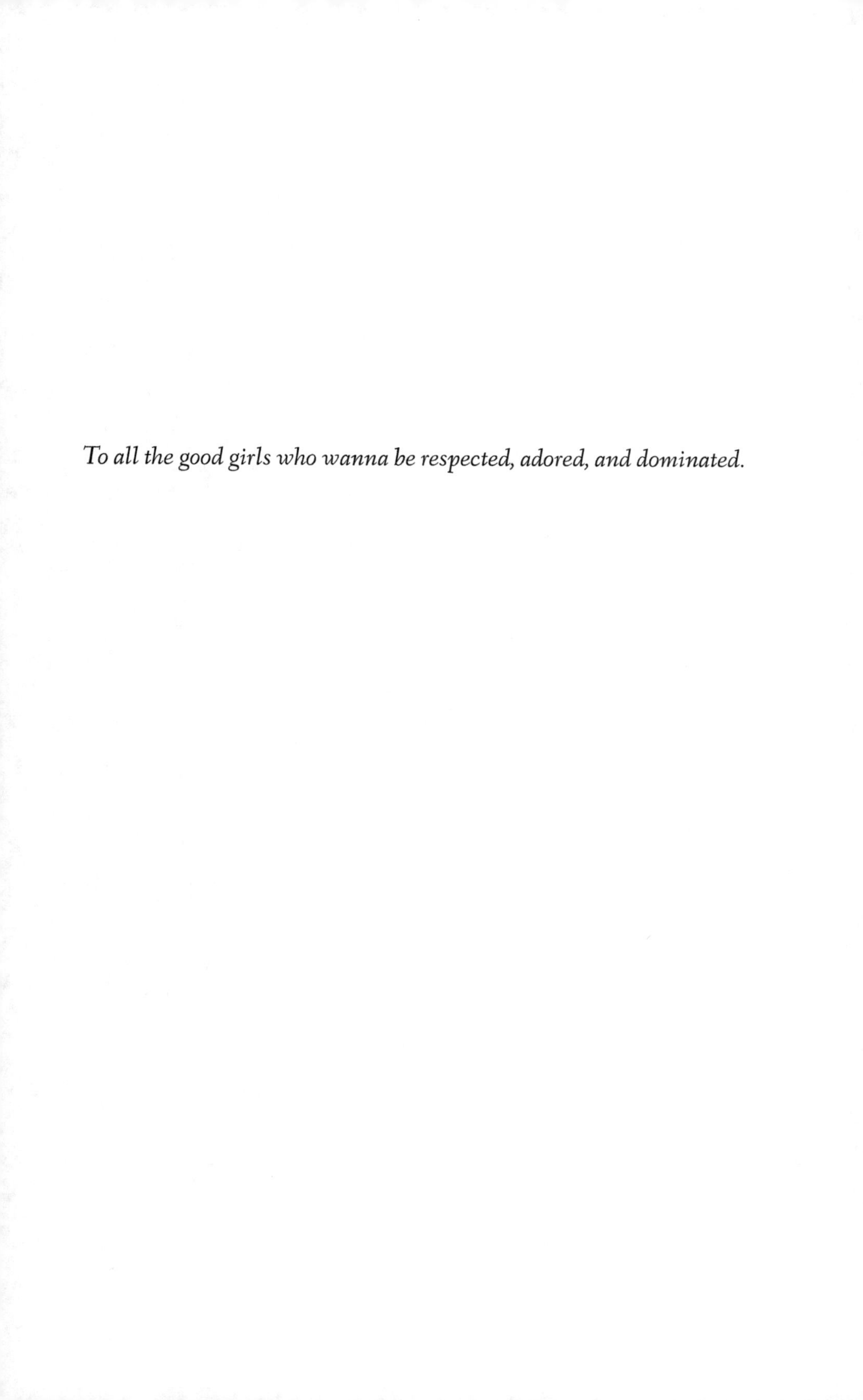

*To all the good girls who wanna be respected, adored, and dominated.*

*"This is a story of a famous dog. For the dog that chases its tail will be busy."*

*–George Clinton*

# Prologue

## What These Bitches Want From a Nigga?

**Jhordyn Davis**

*Ten years ago.*

It was the beginning of summer, two months before the start of my sophomore year. I was nineteen, horny, and sick and tired of being a virgin. All my friends were fucking. Not each other, but you get the point. On the other hand, I was too busy being a biology major with a research internship and a part-time job at the campus library surrounded by shelves of books. There was no time for hanky-panky, college drama, and unwanted pregnancy scares. My tight and demanding schedule literally wouldn't allow me to fuck around.

One day, I was in the dining hall carrying my lunch tray topped with an apple and a Caesar salad from the salad bar when I accidentally bumped into *him*. Jahtavian Amaree Nichols. He was the star receiver for our school's football team and was well-known for his prowess on the field. The earth itself seemed to freeze around him before the apple on the edge of my tray rolled to the floor. We both instinctively reached down to pick it up when our eyes met.

He smiled a lopsided grin at me, and I almost melted into a puddle of lust staring at his sparkling white teeth. He was a gorgeously melanated, six-foot, swaggering creature with an all-American build. His edge-up and tapered fade were fresh around the sides and back of his head, while black curls sprouted from the top of his head. His sparse beard, goatee, and bushy dark eyebrows added character to his already genetically perfect face. He looked like a walking African god, with his *Coppin State Eagles* muscle shirt, gold Cuban link chain, shorts, and backwards fitted *Miami Heat* hat.

In contrast, I was rocking my blue-framed glasses and box braids from spring break in a bun with fuzzed-over triangle parts and inches of textured new growth. I peeled a piece of dressing-drenched lettuce off the front of my T-shirt. An awkward silence hung between us before we burst into laughter.

"Damn, I'm sorry about that. Hope your lunch survived the crash," he acknowledged with a handsome smirk, deepening the dimple on his right cheek.

I smiled back, eyes lingering on his pouty lips for a second too long. "No worries, it's luckily just a fruit casualty and a few pieces of vegetation. I'm Jhordyn, by the way."

"I'm Jahtavian, but everybody calls me Jah. You're in the biology program, right? I've seen you in the science building once or twice."

My brows lifted toward my hairline. I'd always felt invisible on campus. The last thing I expected was to catch the eye of someone on the football team who looked as good as he did. "Yeah, that's me, always buried in lab reports. And you're on the football team. I've seen a few of your games. You're quite the star athlete."

"You noticed lil ol' me out there, huh?"

I giggled. "Yeah. I have."

"So, what's got you on campus over the summer?"

"I'm doing a research internship with Professor Smith and working part-time at the library. What about you?"

"Summer training camp. Got to stay in shape for the season," he replied, flexing his exposed muscles.

The more he talked, the more I giggled, lost somewhere between his sparkling chestnut eyes and his playboy smile. He had me completely under his spell with just one conversation. Jah was the first real dose of social contact I'd had all year. I didn't want our first exchange to be our last. Everything changed when he asked me to grab coffee and suggested we exchange numbers. It was as if my heart had grown wings and fluttered straight out of my chest.

We both pulled out our phones, opened our contacts, and added each other's numbers. Jahtavian even sent a quick text, so we already had a text thread going to schedule a coffee date somewhere between test tubes and touchdowns. We waved goodbye before parting ways. A smile tugged at my lips at the prospect of a budding friendship, or maybe even something more, as the summer nights unraveled.

It turns out that our fateful encounter in the dining hall was just the beginning. As the weeks unfolded, campus became the backdrop to our budding relationship. Jah and I shared laughs and conversations, from the library's quiet corners to the vast football field after practice. We coined ourselves Jah and Jho—nicknames we called each other over texts when we sent memes and funny YouTube and Instagram videos to each other at random times of the day and night.

As the days passed, a noticeable change occurred inside me—a fluttering of my heart, a touch or gaze that lingered a few seconds too long whenever he was in reach, the throbbing between my thighs, a crush unraveling like a spool of yarn. Jah's aura colored my world with the hues of affection, admiration, and lust. Yet, it was a secret whispered only to me. My grandmother would always say *death is nothing, but to live defeated is to die daily*. If I never acted on my feelings, I would never have known if he felt the same way or if things could be more between us by the start of the fall semester.

One night, after grabbing a bite of pizza at a spot near campus, I invited him back to my dorm. *Tonight is the night I feel his lips against mine.* Our sweet first kiss led to private hand-holding and sexting naughty pictures. Soon enough, I gave in to the kisses and imploring in his eyes. Jah took my virginity a week before school started, putting the period at the end of the most romantic summer I'd ever had. Everything was perfect. I remember waking up the following morning with a permanent smile just thinking about what he said and how gentle and attentive he was to my needs. I'd never felt closer to another human being. The dick was immaculate, long, and thick, with a slight curve to the left. Surprisingly, I enjoyed the pain that came with being penetrated. I couldn't wait to feel him inside me again and learn how to please him the way he wanted to be pleased.

But, in proper asshole fashion, he ghosted my ass. Jahtavian went from responding within seconds to leaving my texts on read, dodging me after football practice, and looking right through me in the dining hall as if I'd died and become invisible. It was the most painful, humiliating, rudest awakening I'd ever experienced. I'd gone from floating on cloud nine to burning in the depths of hell.

I caught him alone after practice one evening and confronted him with tears in my eyes. I wanted him to see how broken I'd become in his hands. Instead of apologizing or owning up to his actions like a real man, he crushed my entire world with seven simple words: *We had a fun run. We good?*

That was my introduction to the real world. It was a moment etched so deep into my brain that I'd never forget it. A couple of days after he officially ended things to my face, I found out my grandmother passed away after a long battle with cancer. As her only grandchild, naturally, I was a mess. I wanted to find solace in his arms and maybe even figure out why he'd done what he did. I was even willing to forgive him, all in the name of not being alone and having to deal with two heartbreaks at once. I texted him to let him know she'd passed and called three times before he had the audacity to block me. Turns out, he had an ego as big as his dick, maybe even bigger. Despite my misery, I had to fly back to Houston to be with my family and grieve the loss of my grandmother.

When I returned to Baltimore a few weeks later, word around campus was he'd been sleeping with my roommates. Yes, plural. I lived in an apartment-style dorm with three other females. Jah fucked them all within a matter of weeks. By the time the second semester rolled around, he had transferred schools, moving back to his hometown of Miami. That was the day I became invested in the systematic destruction of Jahtavian Amaree Nichols. I swore on my grandmother's grave he'd regret the day he broke me.

# 1

## Me, Myself & My Obsession

*Present day.*

Have you ever wanted to get your lick back so badly it consumed the darkest corners of your mind? No? Just me. Okay then. But just hear me out before you start judging and turning your nose up and shit. Jahtavian Nichols is a cancer. The toxic, slow-growing kind you never see coming. First, there was me, then my roommates Sequoia and London. He saved Kelsie for last, catching her on a drunken night after a sorority party. He got us all the same way—waited until we were alone or vulnerable, and then swooped in with a smooth pickup line and his famous Captain Save a Ho smile.

I should've seen the signs from the start. Jah was a walking red flag. His kink was meeting a woman with a tight circle of friends and fucking them all one by one. Jah's confidence in his system of juggling women was sickening yet effective. He'd figured out a foolproof way to never get his heart broken, toy with a woman's heart with his charm and fill their heads up with broken promises. Once the panties dropped, he'd disappear like smoke. He got a kick out of watching us turn on each other, changing the dynamic of our friendship underneath one roof. The final act? A teary-eyed crazed bitch telling him how much he wasn't shit. At least, that was my outcome.

I couldn't believe one dick had the power to ruin so much. He tore through our campus apartment like a tornado. For weeks it was like rounds of *Celebrity Death Match* in there with all the screaming and slapping. They were all more experienced than me, and willing to bust it open for the star player on the football team just for a whiff of the attention. It had always been about sex and status with them, but there were real feelings involved and invested time for me.

It took roommate swaps, college transfers, and a hell of a lot of time for us to forgive and see that he was the root of the problem and we'd only been pawns in his game. Today, they've all long since let him go, drowned their *whorrible* decisions in pints of tequila, married men who didn't care about their true body counts, had kids, and moved on with their mediocre lives. After all, it *was* a decade ago. There was a small voice in the back of my mind nagging me to let it go too. *Some niggas will never change. A dog gon' be a dog forever, Jhordyn. Let his flea-bitten ass be somebody else's problem.*

After all, I hadn't laid eyes on him since college—at least not in real life. Online, well, that was another story. Fate landed Jahtavian in my hometown of Houston six years ago. We hadn't had the pleasure of bumping into each other, but I kept a watchful eye from a distance. As badly as I wanted to move on and find a man who respected me, I couldn't. I still wanted Jah to pay for what he'd done to me, what he took from me. It was bigger than my virginity. He'd stripped me of my dignity and left me raw all because I was an easy target.

Like him, most people saw me and thought I was sweet, calm, and maybe even unassuming. But the story you're about to read isn't about me, my wallflower inclinations, and my trust issues toward the opposite sex. No. This is the story of how a toxic ass nigga broke my heart and how I'm about to break his right the fuck back.

---

I SAT AGAINST THE FAR WALL ON THE PLUSH, EMERALD GREEN, velvet sofa, sipping some chamomile tea while lazily scrolling through Jah's Instagram page from my Finsta account. The more I scrolled, the more I felt the familiar dark presence envelop me, whispering venomous encouragement. Inside my mind, where nobody could judge me, I plotted revenge. I'd studied Sun Tzu's *The Art of War* from cover to cover, soaking in as much warfare knowledge as possible because it was precisely that—war. Sun Tzu said: *"If you know the enemy and know yourself, you need not fear the result of a hundred battles. If you know yourself but not the enemy, for every victory gained, you will also suffer a defeat. If you know neither the enemy nor yourself, you will succumb in every battle."*

My thoughts twisted as I looked at him smiling with his coworkers—all heroic, handsome firefighters. His social profiles were a mix of thirst traps of his shirtless, heat-tinged body in his uniform, him in the gym kissing his bulging muscles, and heroic posts that made him go viral for saving lives, coining the viral hashtag, *#HeatHunk.* I rolled my eyes. Of course, he had to go into a noble profession like firefighting and look like a melanated god doing it.

"Fuck boy turned firefighter, who would've thought," I muttered before sipping my tea.

I paused when I saw a moving day video on his Instagram Story. A little cyber-sleuthing showed me that there were multiple available apartments in the new building he'd agreed to call home, even one on his floor right next door. *Holy shit. The stars have finally fucking aligned, Jhordyn.* I looked around the living room of the house my grandmother willed to me after she passed. I'd officially moved in after grad school and had been doing minor renovations here and there when my budget allowed. The walls were a soothing shade of dusty rose, reminiscent of her favorite flower. It was a color that wrapped around me like a warm hug every time I sailed into the room. The dated wooden floorboards were a mix of honey oak and mahogany.

A few potted plants, ferns, and succulents were positioned near the window, basking in the sunlight. Next to the window was an antique wingback armchair. It had to be two decades older than I was, but it wore its age gracefully just like the black woman who'd owned it. The fireplace was lined with built-in bookshelves housing my collection of old biology textbooks, research journals, and a few of my grandmother's cherished photo albums. A cluster of lavender and rose-scented candles sat on the mantel. Their soft glow danced in the evenings, casting eerie shadows across the walls.

Lastly, I looked at the toolbox by the kitchen's entrance. I'd already peeled off layers of wallpaper, discovering a faded floral pattern beneath. I had contractors coming in to finally start the renovations on the kitchen, knock out the wall to open up the space, renovate my master bathroom, and sand and paint the wooden window frames. I'd initially planned to stay in the house while the renovations were taking place, but I made a huge decision once I came across that available apartment. *Revenge will be mine. I'm going to make Jahtavian Nichols pay me back in shattered pieces of his broken heart. I'll make him wish he'd never, ever played in my face.*

Before moving out, I started making changes—switching up my hair, buying a few new pieces of sexy lingerie, and new clothes. I wasn't the same nineteen-year-old girl he'd fucked and forgotten. When I was done with him, Jahtavian Nichols would be the one sitting on the wrong side of a love song.

# 2

## Neighbors Know My Name

*"Attack him where he is unprepared. Appear where you are not expected."*
*-Sun Tzu, The Art of War*

My move-in day rolled around quicker than expected. The best part was that it put me twenty minutes closer to work. I'd put my biology degree to good use, working as a clinical lab scientist at the Houston Medical Center. I made good money and had a massive chunk of change in my savings account from being so frugal over the years and a bit leftover from the inheritance I got from my grandmother, so I hired movers to make my temporary move easier.

"Careful, that's vintage!" I hissed, supervising them from the middle of my empty one-bedroom apartment.

My new luxury high-rise residence was in downtown Houston's historic Market Square district. I'd never been one to splurge, but I could get used to the sleek kitchen and spacious living room—not to mention the state-of-the-art fitness center and resort-style pool. As soon as I stepped through the front door, I was greeted by a spacious foyer with polished hardwood floors. The walls were freshly painted in a shade of eggshell. The movers had already assembled and placed my shoe rack by the front door, ready to organize my mini collection of stylish heels and running shoes.

The sizable living room was flooded with natural light from the floor-to-ceiling windows. I'd chosen the apartment to be closer to Jah, but the stunning city skyline views weren't bad either. My grandmother's vintage emerald green sofa sat against the main wall, adorned with vibrant orange and yellow throw pillows. Across from it were a couple of movers assembling my new TV stand and placing the flat-screen TV on top. I picked up a tote and carried it into the kitchen, which was stacked with dark wood cabinets and white quartz countertops.

I marched down the hall and inside my bedroom where my queen-sized bed dominated the room. I stepped to the side as another mover carried in my dresser and nightstand. A full-length mirror leaned against the wall, reflecting the sunlight streaming through the big window. Perhaps my favorite part of all was my walk-in closet. Even in an apartment, it was the closet of my dreams. There were dozens of racks for my clothes, shelving for shoes, and drawers for my jewelry and accessories.

The bathroom was spa-like. White subway tiles lined the shower, and a rainfall showerhead hung overhead. I arranged my toiletries on the marble countertop before setting up my bathmat and shower curtain. Although I wouldn't be there long-term, I still wanted the place to feel like home. So, I placed a few lavender and vanilla-scented candles by the tub to create a relaxing atmosphere, draped purple fairy lights across my bedroom dresser and the balcony railing, and added a few well-placed indoor snake plants and ferns to breathe life into the space.

I'd spent the last few weeks mapping out Jah's forecasted heartbreak timeline parallel to my eight-week home renovation. The plan was to make him fall in love with me and then yank all his hopes and dreams right from underneath him, breaking his heart in the process. I'd also settled on where to do it, a unique place in the area called Milk & Honey. It was a place a man like Jah would probably *never* go to. But that was for later.

I stepped off the elevator carrying a clear tote labeled "Kitchen" down the hall, balancing it against my hip. Even with help, the move had been exhausting, but I was determined to finish making my new place feel like me. As I approached my open door, I saw Jah step out of the neighboring unit with a smile. It was my first time seeing him in person since college. Online didn't do him justice. His black ass was still as handsome as ever. It almost took my breath away. He wore basketball shorts and a muscle shirt, similar to what he'd been wearing the first time we met in the dining hall. There was a half-second glitch in my step when I noticed him noticing me, but I kept my poker face on.

"Yo, you need some help with that, gorgeous?" he offered, easing his gym bag off his mountainous shoulder.

I swung my head to the left. "Nope. The movers can handle whatever's left."

"You sure? I know how stressful moving can be. I don't mind being neighborly. I've got a little time on my hands before I hit the gym."

After a few fleeting seconds, I gathered the courage to look him dead in his sparkling chestnut eyes. His once scant beard and goatee were full and dark, wrapping from ear to ear. His mahogany brown arms were covered in black tattoo ink.

I scoffed. It had only been ten seconds, and he was all but putty in my hands. "You don't remember me, do you?" I probed, cocking my head to the side.

He blinked rapidly. "I'm sorry, I–"

"Coppin State," I said, tossing him a bone.

When I mentioned our school, he had a flicker of recognition, which only hardened my resolve to get my revenge.

"Jho? Is that you? Oh shit. How you been, beautiful? It's been a minute," he acknowledged, pulling me into a tight hug.

I felt his washboard abs press against me as my nostrils drew in his scent. *Fuck. All these years, and this nigga still smells like a walking orgasm.* He was as handsome as ever, with his charming smile and easygoing manner, with whiffs of that all-American college football star still hovering over him like a halo.

"Ten years," I stated, pulling away from his embrace.

He shrugged his muscular, tatted shoulders. "Damn. Time flies. You look good, girl."

His eyes swept from my head to my toes, surveying me. I kept my chin high, enhancing my confidence and overall allure. I'd traded in my glasses for Lasik surgery a few years back. My long, dark hair was bone straight, framing my face and sweeping down my C-cup chest. My cut-off jean shorts hugged my curves in all the right places, showing off my sun-kissed, buttery brown skin. My T-shirt was oversized and tied into a ball in the back, showing off the dimples in my lower back.

I glanced at my watch before resting my hand on the indent in my waist. "Sure does. So, you live here?"

"Yeah, right next door, apparently. I moved in a few weeks ago."

"Guess that means we're neighbors. I just got my keys today."

"That's wassup. How you been?"

I shrugged my lean shoulders. "Maintaining."

"I hear that. You new to the city?"

"No. Houston's my hometown. I moved back here after grad school. You?"

"I've been here for about six years. I'm a firefighter with the Houston FD at Station Forty-Seven," he boasted with a smile.

My brows quickly rose and fell. I wasn't going to give him the satisfaction of excitement. "Cool," I answered, pretending I didn't already know he pulled three twenty-four-hour shifts weekly.

"You excited to get settled in?" he inquired, dragging out our conversation.

I dipped my chin before glancing at my watch as if I had somewhere better to be. "Yeah."

"You sure you don't need me to put anything together for you or carry in any more boxes?" he offered.

I shook my head, brushing off his help one last time. "Nope. Again, movers."

"Right. If you need anything, furniture assembly or a cup of sugar, just knock."

"Thanks."

"Maybe we can catch up once you're settled, y'know, grab a drink or something."

"Sorry. I'm not interested. Besides, my man wouldn't like that."

His eyebrow lurched toward his crisp hairline. "Your man don't let you have friends?"

I rolled my eyes, ignoring his comment. "I'm sure your girl wouldn't like us catching up."

"How you know I got a girl?" he challenged.

I titled my head to the side. "You just told me."

He smirked. "Slick. But we're old friends, right? Nothing wrong with two friends catching up."

"*Friends*?" I scoffed. "Right. Um, I gotta go. Bye."

"Think about my offer," he called out. "Maybe we could get together over the weekend."

I turned away slowly, making sure to give him the full view of the back of me. "Mmhm, yeah, maybe," I answered before slamming the door behind me.

As I stepped into my new apartment, I couldn't help but smile.

My move was more than just a temporary change of address. It was a chance to make sure his charming smile faltered and that he never, *ever* took advantage of another woman again.

---

It started with moans at three o'clock in the morning.

*"Mmm, shit. Yeah, baby. Right there! Don't stop."*

Then the knocking—the incessant fucking knocking.

My eyes popped open, fixated on the ceiling fan whirring over top my head as I listened to Jah's headboard thump and bang against our shared wall as if we were at Battle of the Bands. The pleasure-filled sounds of another female's nearing orgasm had me ready to climb the walls. The luxury apartment may have been nice, but like most new constructions, the walls were paper-thin. As annoyed and disgusted as I was with the knock-knock, knocking on the wall, a part of me became turned on. Soon enough, I found my hands between my parted thighs and underneath my panties, slowly stroking my hairless sweet spot. I closed my eyes and imagined all the nasty, freaky things he was probably doing to her on the other side of that wall.

I licked my fingertips before placing my hand back in between my legs and permitting my dirty imagination to take me to a place where my fingers weren't my own. They were *his*. After all, he was the reason I'd learned how to please myself and vowed to protect my heart and my body until marriage. I slid my panties to the side and finger fucked myself for pleasure, breathing heavily as I pushed two fingers deep inside me.

I panted. "Mmm, fuck."

Over the years, I'd learned the ins and outs of my body. My fingers were musicians stroking the right keys to make my body buck and shake with pleasure. I bit down on my bottom lip, fucking myself to the same cadence as his thumping headboard. It drove me crazy how turned on I was. I tugged at my nipple, plowing harder as my legs sat wide apart and my toes curled like birthday ribbon. My hand snaked down my body to caress my clit in small circles while I fingered myself with two fingers from the other. My eyes clamped shut, focusing on the building sensation between my legs as I winded my hips underneath the sheets.

I tossed my head back against the pillows, eyes popping wide as my back arched toward the ceiling. "Oooh yeah. Mmm shit! Yes!"

As soon as I came, I got up to take a shower. Panting heavily, I peeled off my creamy, soaked panties, making sure to keep them nearby. I had special plans in mind for them.

I was surprised to hear the knocking continued post-shower. *That nigga's like the fuckin' Energizer Bunny.* The longer Jah fucked, the more the wheels inside my mind churned. The fact that Jah had alluded to having a girlfriend led me to unlock my phone and spiral down an unexpected rabbit hole to find out who the hell she was and if the woman getting her back blown out next door was her or some other know-nothing broad. None of my months of cyber sleuthing had ever uncovered anything about him being in a relationship—not a committed one, at least. So yeah, I wanted to know who he was fucking.

I continued to dig until I finally got so tired that my eyes were going crossed. "Hey, Siri, set a reminder for me to change my room around," I mumbled before passing out about half an hour before sunrise.

---

I STATIONED MYSELF OUTSIDE JAH'S APARTMENT THE NEXT DAY wearing a loose-fitting, white dress shirt with a lapel collar and Chucks. My heart thumped wildly against my ribcage. I was desperate for batteries for my TV remote, which resulted in knocking on his door instead of wasting gas by running out to the store for one thing.

A few seconds passed before the door cracked open, revealing

Jah's amused expression. His eyes widened when he saw me. "Jhordyn. Wassup, gorgeous?" he quizzed, looking me up and down as he licked his lips.

"I need double-A batteries."

He cut his eyes at me with a hint of mischief in his gleam. "Batteries, eh? Whatchu need batteries for? A lil solo play?"

I rolled my eyes. "Batteries, nigga. Don't waste my time. You got them or not?"

He stepped aside, inviting me in. From the glimmer in his eyes, I could tell he was already a little obsessed with me. "Sure, come on in. Let me see what I got for your rude ass."

I arched one of my perfectly sculpted eyebrows. "Thanks."

Jah disappeared down the hall, leaving me alone in his cozy living room. The stylish floor lamp next to the sofa, the sparkling clean stainless steel kitchen appliances, and the small breakfast nook by the window—his tastes had really evolved over the years. I continued to study his style as archaic memories of our summer fling came flooding back, from the posters on his dorm room walls and mine, to the shelves of books we'd make out against during my shifts at the library.

As I sank into the plush couch, I quickly shoved my hand inside my shirt pocket and slipped my panties between the cushions. All I had to do was sit back and wait for my plan to unfold, and pray I was there with popcorn in hand when the fireworks popped off. Just as Jah returned with a handful of double-A batteries, a slow smile spread across my face. He passed them to me.

"Thanks," I said, purposely avoiding eye contact with him. He sat down next to me, closer than necessary, and I sprang to my feet. "Well, gotta go."

My heart skipped a beat as I sailed to the door.

"If you ever need anything else, you know where to find me," he called out.

I tossed him the peace sign over my shoulder. "Noted."

# 3

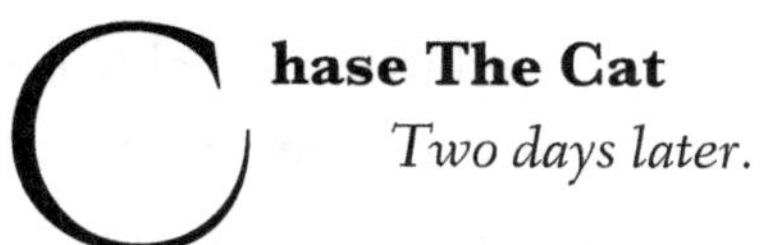

**hase The Cat**

*Two days later.*

*"Hold out baits to entice the enemy. Feign disorder and crush him."*
*-Sun Tzu*

I STEPPED OFF THE ELEVATOR, BALANCING MY GROCERY BAGS AS I trekked toward my unit. My sneakers squeaked against the floor, echoing in the quiet hallway. I'd had a day from hell at work and couldn't wait to unwind with a hot shower and a glass of wine. I heard a commotion inside Jah's apartment as I approached my door. The voices grew louder, punctuated by angry accusations. I slowed down, my curiosity piqued. Seconds later, his door flew open, sending Jah and his alleged girlfriend spilling into the hallway. His eyes quickly darted to me before uncomfortably brushing his hand down the back of his fade. The woman's brown face was flushed with anger, her finger jabbing the center of his chest.

"Eyes here, nigga! You're fucking other bitches, aren't you?" Her voice cracked before she smacked her lips in aggravation.

"No!" he exploded. "How many times I gotta tell you I don't know what the hell you're talking about!"

"Whose fuckin' panties are these, nigga? I know you be havin' all kinds of stank ass hos runnin' through here when I'm not around!"

His expression shifted from shock to annoyance. "Chessy, it's not what you think," he protested.

But before he could explain further, her light-brown hand swung through the air, connecting with his cheek. The stinging snap of her slap echoed down the hall, and he staggered back, his eyes ballooning with shock.

I dipped my chin, stifling a laugh as my keys jingled in the lock. It was a proven fact that toxic niggas *always* wanted to have their cake and eat it too. Watching his drama play out in real time was better than any reality TV show. All I had to do was sprinkle a little razzle dazzle to stir the pot, and the rest did itself. It was all too priceless.

He grunted, regaining his composure after the slap. "I'm telling you, I don't know where they came from! I thought they were yours!"

She scoffed before throwing the panties in his face. "Stay the fuck out of my life!"

I quickly unlocked my door and stepped inside, groceries in tow. The calming aroma of my lavender-scented candles enveloped me as I set the bags on the kitchen counter. My heart raced from the unexpected spectacle in the hallway. It was just the pick-me-up I needed after a long, hectic workday. I recognized that woman's rage all too clearly—that fiery, uncontrollable, all-consuming rage. Jah still had the same dumb-ass, bewildered expression on his face whenever he was forced to tell the truth. I felt the second-hand embarrassment for his ass, only because I'd been the one who planted the panties.

My Echo Dot sat on the edge of my TV stand, its blue ring

glowing as I tapped it. "Alexa, play "Irreplaceable" by Beyoncé," I commanded.

Soon enough, her southern, sultry voice filled the space. *"To the left, to the left, everything you own in the box to the left..."*

A grin spread across my face as I happily swayed to the beat. I twirled in the middle of my living room like a ballerina at center stage. The victory dance was my guilty pleasure—celebrating my silent win. I glanced at the wall that separated Jah's apartment from mine. Blowing up Jah's love life and being there to witness the drama firsthand was the perfect ending to my otherwise mundane Wednesday evening.

---

A FEW MORE DAYS PASSED BEFORE I BUMPED INTO JAH AGAIN. IT was on the running trail at the park near our complex that time. I'd bent down to tie my running shoe when he zoomed past me. He halted his wide-legged stride before spinning around and jogging back toward me.

"Wassup, neighbor?"

"You tell me. How's the cheek?" I quizzed, making him relive the harsh smack I'd witnessed.

"Ouch. I forgot you saw that. Not my finest moment."

I stood, pulling down my tiny running shorts. "I don't know about that. I was thoroughly entertained."

A laugh blew through his nostrils as he surveyed me—from the messy bun on my head to my matching Under Armour sports bra and shorts. "You're ice cold, Jho."

I shrugged off his comment as my thoughts churned. He wasn't wrong. I wasn't the same young, naive, slightly desperate young woman he'd had his way with once upon a time. Thanks to him, I'd learned a lot about the world and how self-absorbed the people in it could be. Jahtavian was a charming devil, no doubt. His unforgettable dimpled smile and the way his seductive brown eyes crinkled each time he laughed—it all tugged at my heartstrings and made my pussy thump. But our college run had a bitter end. I shifted my gaze to the overarching branches that formed a canopy above us. Runners passed by, their nods and half-smiles creating a sense of fellowship amongst us, even if we were all strangers.

"I gotta get back to my run," I stated after finally deciding to grace him with a response.

"What's the rush?" he inquired. "You don't wanna stop and smell the roses?"

I swung my head in a no. "I don't like roses."

"Every woman likes roses."

"Not this one."

"Then what do you like?"

"Sunflowers."

He shrugged lazily. "I guess those are dope."

"Did you know one sunflower is actually thousands of tinier flowers? They can self-pollinate and produce a seed."

He dipped his chin with a nod. "Nah. I didn't know that. So, when are we gonna get together so you can teach me more sunflower facts?"

I folded my arms across my chest as a chuckle belted from my lips. "Boy, stop."

"I'm forreal. You know, we can catch up, you can teach me shit. It'll be like old times."

My gaze met his, and I noticed an eyelash on his lower eyelid. "I don't date men I live next door to," I answered before gently blowing it away from his eye. "It's too messy."

Jah shot me a devilish smirk. "Oh yeah?"

"Yeah. Plus, I got a man, remember?" I reminded him before darting off.

"Damn, so it's like that?" he yelled at my back.

I threw up the peace sign over my head and kept running. As my sneakers rhythmically tapped the ground, my dark thoughts flowed freely. So far, I'd led him on, delayed plans to get together and "catch up," and planted the panties that ultimately destroyed his most recent relationship. My thoughts raced alongside my rhythmic steps, replaying our demise—the tearful, vengeful goodbye when his ass *finally* had the nerve to end things to my face. I'd been a pushover, starstruck that summer I was with him. I knew firsthand if I made things too easy, he'd move on. So, I planned not to show interest. *Keep playing hard to get, Jhordyn. You're doing great.*

Another thirty minutes passed before the path looped back to where I started. My heart clenched as I rounded the bend, the wind tousling the loose strands from my messy bun. I sped up, heading back to my place. My pulse quickened as I neared the building. I slowed my stride and paused nearby to stretch and catch my breath. When I returned to my apartment, sweat-slicked and tired, I noticed the bouquet propped against my door—sunflowers, deep gold and bold orange, wrapped in craft paper. My pulse quickened as I picked up the bouquet and inhaled its sweet aroma. A small note card was tucked inside the paper: *"Did you know sunflowers can also track the sun? Just a lil fun fact I picked up on Google. Teach me more over dinner? - Jah"*

Why the hell was Jah so persistent? Was it remorse? Some misplaced sentimentality behind our not-so-random reunion? Was it a game to him like it was to me? Or was he already that obsessed with trying to get something he couldn't have? I pressed the flowers to my face once again and smiled. The random run-ins, casual invitations, and the surprise sunflower delivery *with* an accurate statistic—Jah had thrown everything at me but the kitchen sink. But I'd mastered the art of evasion, dodging his toxic, repetitive advances like a seasoned pro. I wanted Jahtavian's attention solely on me to the point where he begged me for a date. And from the looks of it, he was like a fish on a hook. I had him right where I wanted him.

"H-HELLO? JHORDYN? CAN YOU HEAR ME?" MY MOTHER ASKED through our FaceTime call.

"Yeah, Mom. I can hear you."

"Why can't I see you?"

I huffed as I pulled the trash bag out of the can and tied it up. "Pull the phone away from your ear, Mom. We're on FaceTime, remember?" I reminded her.

"Oh. Okay. That's better. Can you see me?"

"Yes, Mom," I replied as I left my apartment to head to the dumpster.

Clutching the black trash bag in one hand and my phone in the other, I descended the stairs wearing a faded T-shirt and a high ponytail that tickled my nape. My slippers flopped against the concrete.

"How are the renovations going at Mama's house?" she asked, referring to her childhood home.

"They are going okay. Slow and steady wins the race, I guess," I said with a shrug.

"Other than that, how was your day? I miss you."

I smiled. "Work was work, but other than that, my day was okay. I miss you, too. When are you and Daddy going to come back down to Houston for a visit?"

"After all your renovations are done. You know I can't stand all that dust with my allergies," she complained.

As I reached the communal dumpsters, I noticed Jah near the brick wall with his own bag. His eyes caught the light, crinkling as he looked up from his phone and shot me a disarming smile. My heartbeat quickened.

"Oh, hey, Mom. I gotta go. I'll call you back," I blurted before quickly ending the call.

"Wassup, Jhordyn," he greeted me, his voice smooth as a saxophone riff.

"'Sup?"

"What you up to?"

"Just got off the phone with my mom." I chuckled, thinking about our brief call. "I love her, but she still hasn't mastered how to flip the camera around or remember to hold the phone up to her face instead of her ear whenever she calls me."

He laughed alongside me. "My parents are the same way. My mom is more with the times than my father is, though. For real, my dad is still old school. He's anti-iPhone, anti-technology, and all that."

"Oh no."

"Hell yeah. Hey, you got a second? I wanna holla at you about something."

I sucked my teeth, softening toward him as I flung my bag into the trash bin. "You got three seconds. Wassup?"

"I got a problem."

"Mmm, and what's that?"

"I like this girl, but she doesn't seem to know I'm alive, or at least give a fuck."

I shrugged. "Maybe she isn't the one for you."

He smacked his lips before stroking his beard. "Nah, see, I refuse to believe that. This girl, we got history. She's special."

I scoffed. "Special, huh? Yeah. I bet."

"Yo, wassup with you, Jho? You've been trying to play me ever since you moved in."

"I thought I told you at the park I don't date neighbors? Besides, asshole isn't my type."

His brows shot toward his hairline. "Whoa! Asshole? What did I do to deserve all that?"

I huffed, cocking my head to the side. "Do you remember the last thing you said to me in college?"

He swiped his hand down the back of his fade while looking at the pavement. "Nah. Knowin' me back then, it was probably something wild."

"You said, and I quote, *'We had a good run. We good?'*"

His lips slid to the side in embarrassment while he massaged the back of his neck. "Damn."

"Yeah."

"I apologize. I've grown a lot since then."

"I can't tell."

"Damn," he said, clutching his chest as if he was offended. "You not even gon' give a nigga the benefit of the doubt?"

"You still have yet to give me a reason why I should," I replied, pinning my arms across my chest.

"The flowers don't count?"

"What? What flowers?" I asked, playing clueless.

He sucked his teeth. "C'mon, Jhordyn. Stop fuckin' with me."

I rolled my eyes. "Fuckin' with you? You sound a lil' detached from reality, Jah. The sunflowers I got earlier were clearly from my man."

His tone and his stance shifted. "Your man? They were from me, Jhordyn. There should've been a card."

"You? Why would you, of all people, send me flowers?"

"Maybe I wanted to apologize."

"Um, I heard the argument and saw your girl channel her inner Will Smith before she slapped the shit out of you, remember? I'm not the one you need to be apologizing to. Or at least not the only one."

Jah shook his head. "I wasn't serious about her anyway."

"Mmmm. Of course, you weren't."

"Speaking of your man, where's he at? I ain't seen him around."

"So you're watching me now?" I probed, baiting him.

His brows furrowed. "What? No. I'm not saying that. I'm just saying—you know what, never mind."

A light chuckle slipped past my lips. "Yeah. I think you should stop while you're ahead. It's giving Creep Squad."

His gaze lingered on my face. "Let me take you to dinner and show you how much I've changed."

"What part of *I have a man* don't you understand, or do you still have zero morals?"

I'd spent years building a wall around myself, brick by brick, fortified by independence and the resolve to get my revenge. Yet, Jah's constant presence started chipping away at my defenses just like it had done all those years ago.

"You know I'ma keep asking until you say yes, right? All you gotta do is say the magic word to get me to stop."

"What's that? Police?"

He scoffed, which made me laugh. "At least let me put my number in your phone."

"Oops. Too bad I don't have it on me."

"Then, put your number in mine," he said before passing it to me. "I'll only use it for emergencies. After all, we *are* neighbors."

"Sure. Whatever." I extended my hand, feeling a jolt of electricity when our fingers briefly touched. I plugged in my number and passed it back to him. "Just know if you get out of hand, I will block your ass," I warned.

He chuckled. "Chill."

I turned to walk back into the building. "Bye, Jahtavian."

"Hey, yo. Hold up. On a serious note, I've been meaning to tell you I'm sorry about your grandmother."

I froze. His sincerity had completely caught me off guard. "W-what did you say?"

"I know I didn't handle things well back then, especially not when it had to do with death. It's kind of ironic now that I'm a firefighter and see death so much. But I just wanted to make sure I said that."

I cleared my throat. I hadn't expected Jah's spontaneous apology or acknowledgment of his wrongs, but something about his sincerity reeled me in. My breath caught in my throat, and the air suddenly felt thinner than usual. I'd spent so much time studying the bad parts of him so that he wouldn't knock me off my square that his genuineness had sent me on an emotional rollercoaster ride I hadn't prepared for.

"Um, thanks. I didn't think you remembered that."

"Yeah, well, your comment about the last thing I said to you got me thinking."

"Right."

"You know, I've also been meaning to ask, do you like karaoke?" he probed, switching to a lighter subject.

I raised a questioning eyebrow. "Why? Are you challenging me to a sing-off?"

He grinned. "Maybe. There's a karaoke bar nearby. Live music, dim lights—it's a vibe. Me and my family from the station go sometimes after shift."

"I do sing a mean version of Beyonce's "Love on Top" in the shower," I admitted.

His eyes sparkled. "Bet. I'll hit you up the next time we go."

"Sure. Goodnight for real this time."

"Night."

# 4

## Old Dog, New Tricks

*"At first, then, exhibit the coyness of a maiden until the enemy gives you an opening; afterward, emulate the rapidity of a running hare, and it will be too late for the enemy to oppose you."*
*-Sun Tzu*

I finally let Jah convince me to join him for drinks and a song at the karaoke bar. He'd practically begged me to, so I had to put the poor boy out of his misery. The softly lit karaoke bar hummed with excitement. Velvet, red curtains decorated the entrance, muffling the bustling sounds of the city outside its doors. The scent of tequila and excitement filled the space as laughter and music echoed off the walls.

I glanced at my text to reference which karaoke room to meet Jah. "Karaoke Room number five," I mumbled just before stepping inside.

The room was cozy, decorated with black chalkboard walls filled with signatures, funny sayings, positive affirmations from past guests, and a couple of cocktail tables and plush leather couches. An old-school mic stood in the center of the small stage, awaiting the next performer. Above, fairy lights were draped across the ceiling, casting a soft glow. I looked around, searching for Jah amongst the male and female firefighters filling the space. Our eyes connected simultaneously, and a soft smirk lifted one side of his mouth. He still had that charming, boyish smile and was still smooth as silk, but all of that was a mark against him as far as I was concerned.

"You made it," he commented when he approached me.

I gave him a onceover. He was clad in all black with a gold Cuban link chain around his neck. His look complemented mine. I wore a black one-shoulder blouse with matching high-waisted skinny jeans. My Gucci belt with the double G's adorned my waist, and cut-out gold heels were strapped to my feet. "Yup."

"Can I get you a drink?"

"I'm gonna need one if you expect me to get up on that stage and sing in front of all these people," I replied.

"What are you drinking?"

I smirked. "A shot of tequila or two."

A grin creased his face. "Bet. Have a seat. My table is right over there," he said, pointing to the cocktail table to the left of the stage."

"Okay."

He walked away before turning around. "You're wearing the hell out of that outfit, by the way." He complimented me with a wink before heading to the bar.

I stifled a smirk as I stalked to the table, heels clicking against the floor. The room was filled with a melting pot of seasoned veterans who'd been at the station for years and fresh recruits from the academy. I gave audience to their stories about firehouse pranks, toy drives, calendar fundraisers, and chili cook-offs. It was a family held together tight like glue.

A burly Hispanic man with a salt-and-pepper beard approached me with a smile. "You must be Nichols' lady," he acknowledged, reaching to shake my hand. "I'm Captain Hernandez. He's one of our best."

I shook his hand as another woman with kind blue eyes joined us. "I'm not his lady. I'm just his neighbor. Nice to meet you, though. My name is Jhordyn."

"Are we talking about Nichols?" the petite woman asked.

"Yup," Captain replied.

"Did Captain tell you about the save Nichols had a few months ago? He saved a little girl from a burning apartment building."

My brows heightened, unable to picture Jah running into a burning building, although I knew that was part of the territory. "Seriously?"

She dipped her chin with a nod. "Sure did. Flames were dancing in the sky when we charged in. He found a little girl, maybe about nine or ten, trapped on the fifth floor."

"That was a tough call," the Captain recalled.

"Yeah, and Nichols didn't hesitate for a second, even when the stairs collapsed."

I slapped my hand over my mouth. "Hold up. The stairs collapsed?"

"He saved her, though. I'm just glad they both made it out alive," the woman added.

"And Nichols took it all in stride. But between us, I talked to the Chief about him. They're considering him for a Medal of Valor award for that rescue."

My heart swelled with excitement as if I'd been named the award winner. "Wow, what an honor."

I'd seen Jah's player side, even the playful and asshole sides of his multifaceted personality, but hearing the story of his bravery and care made my hard edges soften. Before our conversation continued, Jah approached with our drinks in hand. "Here you go," he said, passing me my double shot of tequila. "What are y'all talking about?"

"You," I answered.

"I was telling her about your big save a few months back," the woman told him.

Jah shook his head. "C'mon, Liz, you're embarrassing me."

She playfully nudged him. "You're a hero, Nichols. Get used to it."

Captain Hernandez clapped Jah on the back of his shoulder. "Keep it up, Nichols."

Jah sat beside me and placed his hand on my thigh. "I'm glad you came."

I shot him a playful smirk before lightly pushing his hand away. "Seeing you get up on that stage and embarrass yourself? Oh, I wouldn't miss it for the world."

---

As THE NIGHT PROGRESSED, WE SAT AND WATCHED HIS coworkers drink and sing off-key into the mic when Jah excused himself. I nodded while sipping my tequila sunrise cocktail, wondering where he'd gone. When the song ended, I looked up to see Jah standing on the stage holding the microphone.

Jah cleared his throat, and the room fell silent. "This one goes out to the pretty girl over there," he said, his voice steady as his eyes locked on mine.

The music to his song selection started playing, and I glanced at the monitor displaying the lyrics to "All The Things (Your Man Won't Do)" by Joe. Jah began to sing, his baritone voice a sultry blend of honey and vulnerability. The entire room seemed to blur as he crooned, making my heart skip a beat. I couldn't pry my eyes away from him.

By the second verse, he stepped off the stage and came down to my table to grab my hand as he sang to me. My eyes bugged. Jah's surprise serenade was the last thing I expected. If there had been a sinkhole in the floor, I would've gladly volunteered to be the first to get sucked in. His soothing, melodic voice enveloped me like a warm hug. *Don't do it, Jhordyn. Don't fall for this nigga twice.*

When the last note hung in the air, Jah returned to the stage, allowing me the chance to bolt. The crowd cheered as I rushed out of the room, desperate for fresh air. I felt a nauseating mix of surprise, flattery, and affection toward Jah, all while feeling like the walls would close in on me at any moment. I couldn't stop my heart from fluttering with the unexpected excitement from his romantic gesture. There was too much vulnerability and effort behind it for it to be an act, right? Or maybe serenading bitches in public settings was his new kink.

We both knew Jah was banking on his charm to get me into bed. What he didn't realize was that I wasn't that easily swayed. He still used his devilishly alluring smile, dreamy bedroom eyes, and melodic voice to get what he wanted. Sure, the sexual tension was there between us. Had my pussy been calling the shots, I would've given into him on sight. I hated to admit there was a small part of me that wanted to give in to him, but I refused to be used like that again. I couldn't be.

I rested my hand on my chest, trying to slow my heart rate, when I heard his familiar voice behind me. "Jhordyn, are you okay?"

"I'm fine," I answered without turning to face him.

"Why'd you run out like that?" he asked, inching closer.

I turned to face him. "That was... a lot."

His brows shifted downward. "You didn't like it?"

"Why didn't you ever tell me you could sing?" I questioned.

His muscular shoulders rose and fell. "It's one of my many hidden talents. I just don't lead with it."

"Well, maybe you should."

"I thought you didn't like it?"

"I never said that."

He huffed. "You never said you did either. I mean, damn, Jhordyn. Trying to impress you is terrifying as hell. Why is it so hard to get a positive reaction from you?"

"Maybe you should stop trying so hard and start being yourself," I suggested.

"Fine. I'll do whatever you want me to do."

"Yeah?" I asked, voice lifting with excitement.

He dipped his chin. "Yeah."

"Tell me something about yourself nobody else knows, like the singing. I still can't believe I didn't know that about you."

"It's not something I boast about."

"So, you don't go around serenading bitches on the regular?"

Jah cut his eyes at me with a confused brow. "Why would you think that?"

"You know you could charm the rattle off a snake, right?"

"I mean, yeah, but that's not why I did it."

"Then why did you do it?"

"Because I–I don't know. Maybe you're right. Maybe a part of me was trying to impress you."

I scoffed. "That's the first time you've been honest with me all night, maybe even ever."

"I used to sing in the choir growing up," he blurted.

My eyes squinted. "What?"

"You said you wanted to know something nobody else knows, right? Well, there you go."

I snickered. "When? Where? I need details. Because what I'm picturing in my head right now is priceless. Lil' church boy Jah."

"Shut up, yo. My mother was the choir director at our church. I sang in the youth choir until seventh grade. Then, when football got to be too much, I let singing go. But it's like muscle memory. I don't always go around singing, but I can still do my thing."

"I can see that."

"Yeah, well, I bet your man sings to you all the time," he stated.

"Who?" I quizzed, arching a questioning brow in his direction.

"Your man."

I shook my head, realizing what he'd asked too little too late. "Oh. Right. Yeah. Him. I don't know what I thought you said. This liquor got me tripping."

"Are y'all still together?"

"Mmhm," I answered with a nod. "Why wouldn't we be?"

"What's his name again?"

"Why do you care?" I asked before pinging my gaze to the pavement and then over his shoulder.

"What's his name, Jho?"

"It's Davis!" I blurted out, catching the name of a nearby street.

"Davis who?"

"Davis Davison."

"Who?"

"You heard me. His name is Davis Davison."

He sucked his teeth. "That's cap. Stop lying. What kind of fuckin' name is Davis Davison? Are you single or not?"

I huffed, dropping my poorly thought out facade. I'd never expected him to press me so hard about my fictional boyfriend. I hadn't bothered to dream up any real details. I rolled my eyes. "Whatever. So what if I am?"

"So, you sayin' that when I was in there singing to you about all the things I wanted to do that your man wouldn't, and you was sitting over there acting all proud like you was taken by another nigga, that was all cap?"

"I said whatever, nigga! Move on already!"

"Yes or no? I wanna hear you admit it."

"So fucking what!"

He smirked. "Mmmhmm."

"What?"

"Nothing."

"Say it."

"It's nothing."

"Say it or I'm leaving," I threatened.

"Chill. I was just thinking that since you single, you know what that means, right?" he probed, arching a questioning brow.

"What?"

"It means this is technically a date."

I folded my arms across my chest. "Negative, Captain Planet. It's far from a date, okay? This is the most non-date of all dates I've ever dated," I said, twisting my words with frustration.

He chuckled. "Yeah, okay. Whatever helps your pretty ass sleep at night."

I rolled my eyes. "Whatever."

"So, now that this is a date... Are you coming back inside with me?"

I cut him a stern glare that softened by the second. I wanted to hate him, but I couldn't. I still wanted to have that man on his knees, begging to be allowed to have me just *one* more time. So, I played along, knowing I'd get that chance, eventually.

"Fine. Let's go. But you owe me another drink."

---

Jah and I stayed in the karaoke room, sharing a few of his scariest rescue stories and past college memories. He revealed how his father was an EMT and how he'd been a firefighter at his station for almost five years. I confessed my secret love for vinyl R&B records and discussed the high-level details of my job at the medical center. It turns out that we had the same taste in music and sports teams. We both had tickets to the upcoming Houston Rockets game. When he put the idea out there that we should go together, I didn't immediately shut him down.

The fairy lights flickered above us, casting a soft glow against his melanated skin. I stirred my cocktail, my eyes set on Jah. "You know what I've always wondered?"

"What?"

"Why'd you transfer colleges in the middle of the year?"

He shrugged, tracing the rim of his rock glass. "Back then, I was lost. College started to feel like a maze of unrealistic expectations and wrong turns. The pressure, the routine, it was suffocating me, and that was on the football side of things."

"I mean, transferring mid-year was super unusual."

"I needed a fresh start. Somewhere I could breathe."

I nodded. "I get it."

"But seeing you again, I don't know. It feels like a second chance."

"You sound soft as baby shit right now."

He quickly swung his head in a no. "Yo, chill. I'm just saying, you know, as friends."

"Yeah, maybe," I answered.

Part of me expected him to use lines like '*Are your feet tired because you've been running around in my mind all day*' and other cheap pickup lines to get what he wanted, but he didn't. He'd done the opposite and shown me another side of him I never thought existed. I didn't know what that said about him or me. Could a toxic ass nigga like him who'd wreaked so much havoc in my life actually evolve into a decent human being worthy of my companionship? I guess only time would tell.

# 5

## Players Gon' Play

*"Let your plans be dark and impenetrable as night, and when you move, fall like a thunderbolt."*
*-Sun Tzu*

The tomato sauce simmered on the stove as the aroma of spices filled my small kitchen. I stirred the pot of chili while humming along to Fantasia's "Free Yourself" when there was a knock at the door. Curious, I put the lid on the pot before wiping my hands on my kitchen towel and walking to the door. I swung it open to see Jah standing there wearing his matching uniform shirt and blue pants, looking damn good. Seeing him in uniform ignited more than just flames inside me.

"H-hey," I stammered before clearing my throat. "Hey."

"Hey. You got a second? I need a favor."

I raised a questioning brow. "What kind of favor?"

"I got the word earlier today that I'm getting an award."

"The Medal of Valor?"

"Yeah. How'd you know?"

"A little birdy may have mentioned it that night at karaoke."

"Oh?"

"Yeah. Congrats."

He cheesed. "Thank you. It means a lot."

"So, what did you need?"

He ran his hand down the back of his fade, stopping at the nape. "Yeah, so I'm being awarded at the Firemen's Ball this Saturday. It's last-minute, I know, but my family can't make it, and I don't want to accept it alone like a loser."

My brows lifted toward my widow's peak. "You want *me* to be your date?"

"Yeah. I know it's real last minute, but—"

"Uh, yeah. It's Wednesday! I don't have anything to wear. Plus, look at my nails and my hair!"

"I'm sure whatever you pull off will be perfect," Jah encouraged.

My chest deflated with a long sigh. "Okay, fine. I'll go with you."

He cheesed even harder than the first time, dimples prominent in his cheeks. "Word? Thank you! You're a lifesaver, Jho. I mean that. And by the way, whatever you're cooking smells good as hell."

"Oh, that's my grandmother's secret recipe for homemade chili."

"Chili? Oh shit. No disrespect to your grandmother, but don't nobody make a meaner chili than me," he boasted. "My firehouse chili is to die for."

I rolled my eyes. "Yeah, okay. First, you can sing and now you're a chef in the kitchen, too?"

He chuckled. "I'm being forreal. I make it down at the station from time to time. There's hardly ever any left for seconds."

"Well, Mr. Firefighter, you're welcome to stay for dinner and do a taste test," I challenged before realizing what I'd said.

Jah smirked. "I think I might have to take you up on that offer. Let me see what you got going on in here," he said while entering the kitchen.

Jah waltzed over to the pot with me hot on his heels. I smacked his hand as soon as he reached out to grab the lid. "Wash your damn hands first, nasty!"

He tossed his hands up in the air. "You right. My bad, my bad."

Jah walked over to the kitchen sink before soaping and thoroughly washing his hands. He approached the stove with a curious brow and lifted the lid on the pot. "What do you put in yours?"

"The normal stuff—ground beef, red bell peppers, beans, tomato sauce, onions, chili powder, cheese, you know, stuff like that."

"Mmm. What about the cornbread?"

"Baking in the oven as we speak," I answered confidently.

He gave me a nod of approval before spooning a bit into his mouth. "Mmm."

"Well?"

"Needs one thing," he said as his eyes darted around my counter in search of something specific.

"What? What are you looking for?"

"Paprika."

"It's right over there," I answered, pointing to the left side of the counter.

Jah shook the seasoning throughout the pot, dispersing it with the spoon, before putting it to his lips again for a second taste test. "Ah, it's perfect now. Try it," he insisted.

He held his hand under the chili spoonful before holding it to my lips. I gently blew on it before allowing him to feed it to me. My brows heightened as the intense flavors excited my tastebuds. "Mmm."

"Perfect, yeah?"

"So perfect." I agreed with a smirk and a nod.

The weekend rolled around, and my heart fluttered as I smoothed my palms down my long, crimson gown. Attending the Firemen's Ball with Jah hadn't been a part of my plan, but I couldn't ignore the anticipation bubbling up inside me. The door swung open, revealing Jah in his dress uniform—crisp navy blue, gold buttons, and a gold badge that gleamed in the light. I couldn't tear my eyes away. His muscular shoulders, the way the uniform hugged his tall frame, he was a sight that made my entire body light up like a pinball machine.

"Jhordyn," he belted out, voice steady. "You look amazing."

I nervously tore my gaze down to my heels. "Thank you," I responded, cheeks warm as his eyes caught mine. "And you—well, you're every woman's firefighter fantasy come true."

"Yours included?"

I tilted my head before brushing my silky strands behind my ear. "The verdict's still out on that."

"You ready to go?"

"Yeah. Let me grab my clutch."

We hit the elevator arm-in-arm before climbing into his black pickup truck. The engine roared to life, and I held on as we sped toward the ball.

"So, uh, your parents. Why couldn't they come tonight?" I inquired when the truck slowed to a halt at a red light.

He shrugged. "Oh, uh. That's a long story."

"I'm yours for the night, at least the next few hours, so I've got time."

"It's my pops. He's sick—stage three prostate cancer. My mom would've come, but she wouldn't travel without him, and she didn't feel right leaving him home alone. I'm not trippin', though. I understand it."

"Cancer sucks," I replied. "My grandmother passed away from stomach cancer. It got really bad at the end."

Jah dipped his head. "Yeah. I'm sorry to hear that."

"For what it's worth, I'm sorry to hear about your father. They always tell you how hard cancer is on the person suffering from it, but you never hear enough about the family members who are right there going through it with them. It takes a toll on us, too."

He nodded in agreement. "You're right about that."

I reached over and grabbed his hand. "Let's make sure we have a good time tonight for both of them."

He squeezed my hand. "Bet."

---

THE BALLROOM DOORS SWUNG OPEN, REVEALING A SEA OF NAVY blue uniforms and sparkling gowns. The room smelled like cologne and too much hairspray. Jah led me inside, our fingers gently intertwined. The grand ballroom glittered with golden light as firefighters in their dress uniforms mingled with their guests. The soft music swirled around us, and the light scent of fresh red roses from all the centerpieces on the table hung in the air.

We stepped in front of the large backdrop with the Houston Fire Department's emblem and let the professional photographers take our photo. Then, we walked around the silent auction, where cool experiences like a Caribbean cruise and a ride-along in the fire truck were being auctioned. After taking our seats, the fire chief took the stage to deliver a heartfelt opening speech, acknowledging the bravery and dedication of the Houston FD firefighters.

The crowd hushed as he held up the Medal of Valor, representing exceptional bravery. My heart raced as he called Jahtavian's name, and I watched him accept his medal from the front row. At the podium, Jah cleared his throat.

"Thank you," he began. "I share this honor tonight with all my fellow firefighters who run toward danger every single day. It's wild because growing up, I always thought my destiny was to be in the center of a football field underneath those stadium lights with a roaring crowd of fans yelling my name. But life had other plans. When I stepped into the firehouse for the first time, I knew I'd found my purpose.

"A few months back, my team and I faced a raging inferno. Luckily, I was able to save a child, and we all pulled through. I'm grateful I have a team full of amazing firefighters who have my back just as much as I have theirs. Public service has always been in my blood. My father was an EMT, and my mother was an elementary school teacher. And although they couldn't be here tonight, Mom, Dad, this is for you, for teaching me that all heroes don't wear capes. Thank you."

The entire ballroom erupted in applause, and I swiped tears from my eyes as I quickly got to my feet, clapping alongside everyone. Jah's journey, from his football dreams to heroic firefighting, inspired everyone in the room, including me.

Jah stepped down from the stage and back over to our table and kissed my cheek.

"Thanks again for being here."

---

After additional medals were awarded and a tribute to fallen firefighters was given, we were served plated meals and flaming cupcakes for dessert. Soon after, the DJ made the dance floor come alive. Jah and I swayed to the music alongside the other firefighters, their families, and dates.

He pulled me close, our bodies rocking to the beat. "Am I your hero?"

"Maybe for the night."

I'd enjoyed throwing him flirtatious glances and whispering naughty things in his ear as we tore up the dance floor. Watching him slowly going nuclear aroused me to the point where I almost decided to let him have me. As the clock neared midnight, we found ourselves in a quiet corner of the ballroom. The music softened to a slow, soulful melody, and our eyes met. With the warmth of liquid courage and the rekindled spark between us, we leaned in. Our lips met in a tender kiss before I gently pulled away.

"What are we doing?" I whispered against his soft lips.

"Kissing," he answered as his hand grazed my nape, pulling me in for more.

Our second kiss was even more exhilarating than the first. It was as if our lips had become magnets, pulled together by forces greater than us. His tongue plummeted to the depths of my throat, teasing mine with feathery licks.

I purred before gently easing my mouth away from his. "Mmm. Wow."

"What?"

"That was intense," I answered, wiping the corners of my mouth.

He leaned in. "Maybe I like intense."

I pulled back and tilted my head to the side. "You're not getting serious on me, are you?"

"Serious like how?"

"I wanna make sure we're on the same page," I stated.

"And what page is that?"

"The fun page."

"Fun, huh?"

"Yeah."

"It's your world, Jhordyn. Whatever you say goes."

---

We arrived back at my door at the end of the night. Jah was still in his dress uniform as I carried my heels in my left hand. I fumbled with my keys, liquored-up butterflies fluttering around in my stomach.

"You had a good time tonight?"

I nodded with a smile. "I did. Way more than I expected, actually."

"Good. Thanks again for coming with me."

I looked up at him, my gaze lingering on the medal pinned to his chest. Before I knew it, his lips brushed against mine—a leap into the final phase of the evening.

"Jhordyn, I want you—"

I kissed him again before stepping over the threshold, leaving him in the hallway. "I gotta go."

"Can I come in? I don't want the night to end."

A slow breath eased out as I pressed my palm against his chest. "I have a confession."

"What's that?"

"I'm not the same nineteen-year-old girl I was the last time we were together. My tastes aren't as vanilla as they used to be."

"Meaning?" he probed.

"Karaoke dates and sunflowers are cool, but I want something a little... spicier."

"Spicier?"

"Yeah, Jah. You fight fires, right?"

"Yeah."

"Then I take it you know how to make me hot."

He stepped forward, ready to accept the challenge. "How hot you want me to make you?"

"I want you to fuck me publicly and show the world what you have."

He hesitated. "Publicly?"

"I don't want you to fuck me in a McDonald's bathroom or on the balcony of some hotel if that's what you're thinking. That's not what I want at all. I want something thrilling and risqué."

"Risqué?"

"Have you ever been to a club called Milk & Honey?"

"Never heard of it. What's that?"

"It's a sex club."

His brows heightened in surprise. "A what? A sex club?"

"Fuck me there... if you're brave enough."

I slowly pulled away and closed the door in his face. I knew the odds that Jahtavian Nichols had been anywhere near a sex club were slim to none when I brought it up to him. But if he wanted me? He'd have no choice but to meet me there. He just wouldn't know my true scheme.

# 6

## The Land of Milk & Honey

*"The spot where we intend to fight must not be made known; for then the enemy will have to prepare against a possible attack at several different points."*
*-Sun Tzu*

The following week rolled around, and I sent Jah a text with the website of the sex club, Milk & Honey, and the date and time to meet me there. *If he wants me, he'll show up. If not, well, I'll have to devise another plan.* I stepped inside my walk-in closet and pulled out the particular outfit I'd bought online for the occasion—a pair of sexy, black vinyl hot pants and matching bustier. My long hair was filled with voluminous bombshell curls, wild and free, to match my mood, and my lips were painted crimson red. I topped off my risqué ensemble with a black trench coat and red four-inch heels before grabbing my clutch filled with a pair of handcuffs, a flogger, breath mints, and condoms. I took one last look into my floor mirror, skating my hands down my hips. The hot pants I had on showed every curve and contour on my petite body. I was more than ready to show them off and watch Jah drool.

It'd been weeks since I moved in next door, and I kept finding myself thinking about Jah in romantic terms, daydreaming about him like I had when I was that stupid, naive teen. The feelings were all too familiar, and I didn't like that shit. I'd given him my heart and body once before, which got me nowhere. Letting feelings come between the plan I'd curated wasn't good for me, but there was something about him that I couldn't stay away from. *I can't fall for him again. Can I?* If Jahtavian seriously wanted me, that would mean he'd have to be responsible for someone else's feelings other than his own, which I knew he was incapable of doing. He'd fumble sure enough, and I'd be the only one left to pick up the pieces for a second time.

I parked the car, glancing at the time on my screen before I turned off the GPS. It was five minutes until midnight, and my nerves were on a thousand. Everything had been leading up to that moment, but could I pull it off? It was too late to turn back. I had no choice but to find out.

"Tonight is the night you get your revenge, Jhordyn," I mumbled to my reflection in the sun visor mirror before exiting the car.

Milk & Honey was hidden in plain sight on the city's outskirts. From the looks of their website and the limited information I could find about it on the internet, the club was a blend of privacy, relaxation, and indulgence. A strict dress code and an entry fee were enforced. I stepped behind the unmarked door. The walls were dark wood, absorbing whatever light filtered in through the heavy red velvet curtains.

I paid my fee and handed over my cell phone before going down the stairs to the next floor, where the bar was. The air smelled of aged leather, cigar smoke, and a hint of promiscuity. Regulars were perched on plush barstools, their eyes assessing newcomers as if they could sniff us right out. A part of me had expected to walk in and see everyone butt-ass naked and getting busy in the middle of the floor, but everyone I saw had on lingerie, dresses, or business attire and were mingling by the bar or swaying to the music.

The neon-lit bar was filled with every spirit imaginable—from cognac and whiskey to champagne and tequila. Strobe lights flashed by the DJ booth, casting blinking patterns on the mirrored walls. The speakers blared music that assaulted my eardrums in the best way. I smoothed the palms of my hands down the front of my trench coat as I sailed over to the bar. As soon as the bartender handed me my drink, Jah appeared. He wore a V-neck shirt, jeans, and loafers in black from head to toe. His gold Cuban link chain sparkled against his melanated skin and the tattoos on his collarbone. I watched his eyes scan the room before landing on mine. I waved him over with a seductive smirk.

"You showed," I said.

"I told you I would. Midnight though? Why so late?"

"Welcome to my dark side, Jahtavian. I promise you're gonna love it." I chuckled. "You want a drink?"

He nodded before taking a seat beside me. "Hell yeah. How'd you stumble across this place anyway?"

"I told you my sexual tastes are far from vanilla. It's usually members-only, but they let in newcomers every other Friday."

"Which is why we're here?"

"Exactly. I was waiting for the perfect time to try it out, and now just so happens to be it."

He smirked, flexing his dimple. "So, what you're saying is, you wanted to try it out with me?"

I rolled my eyes skyward before sipping my drink. "Simmer down, cowboy. Don't get too ahead of yourself. This is a place where people can explore their kinks and their fantasies in peace. We're just... feeling things out right now. Got it?" I stated, making sure he knew exactly who was in control.

Jah ran his hand down his bearded jawline before dipping his chin. "I already told you it's your world, Jhordyn. I'm here to be used in whatever way you want me."

"You want me to use you, huh? Is that your kink, Jah? Is that what turns you on?" I probed.

He brushed me off with a laugh. "Chill. I was kidding."

I loosened my trench coat so he could glimpse what I had on and leaned closer to squeeze his thigh. "Relax. Whatever happens here stays here," I whispered. "C'mon, let's go."

---

I GRABBED JAH'S HAND AND LED HIM TOWARD THE NEXT FLIGHT of descending stairs. I felt his eyes staring a hole into my back, eager to undress me, but I refused to turn around. The next floor had two stripper poles near a glass wall and a few plush couches and cocktail tables scattered about. I caught Jah's gaze in the mirrored reflection as we moved around the space, eyes soaking in as much as they could. My heart rate increased every time his gaze caught mine. I couldn't wait to see how far I could push him until he couldn't take it anymore. To the back of the room was pornography playing on a projector while a Caucasian man with dark brown hair sat with his trousers around his ankles, freely stroking his stunted dick as he watched.

The next level down was where the magic happened. We kept walking, taking in the sights—a row of women sucking dick, chains and ropes hanging from the walls, couples fucking publicly but as if no one else was there. The more we explored, the kinkier things got. I witnessed group sex play, men on men, women on men, all in the same space. I'd always assumed that voyeurism would make me feel and look like a perv, but the longer I stayed, the more comfortable I became walking through the sea of sex and absorbing the sights.

"Any of this your flavor?" I asked Jah as we stopped to watch two women pleasure each other in a secluded corner.

He gave me a cool shrug. "I mean, it's something."

"Is this turning you on?" I queried, eyeing him closely as I ran my index finger down his chest.

"To be honest, this is not what I expected from you at all."

"What exactly did you expect when you agreed to meet me here tonight?"

"I don't know. You only get so much from the website. It's pretty discrete. To be honest, I came here to kick it with you."

"*Just* kick it?" I probed, not believing him.

His broad shoulders rose and fell. "If kicking it led to me finding out what's really underneath that trench coat, I'd be down for that too."

I smirked. "Mmm. I bet you would. What turns you on, Jahtavian?"

"You," he answered boldly, refusing to shy away from my question.

"Mmm, good answer. Typical, but good."

Finally, I led him to our own private area with only a bed and no door. Although I was in control, I still felt breathless, as if he was breathing down my neck, waiting for me to slip up so he could take the lead. I pushed him against the bed and untied my trench coat before slipping it off and seducing him with light touches.

"What's the most sensitive part of your body? Is it your chest, or maybe something a little lower?" I muttered as I straddled him.

He wasted no time gripping my small waist as he stationed his eyes on mine. "You're the most gorgeous woman I've ever seen. You know that?"

I tilted my head to the left. "Yeah? Tell me something you find incredibly attractive about me that I'd never guess."

"This... *you*, right here, right now. I love seeing this wild side of you. I never knew you had it in you."

"There's a lot of things you don't know about me, Jahtavian."

"I'm willing to learn."

"I bet you are. But tonight isn't about me. Well, not completely. It's about you."

"Why me?"

"Because you, Jahtavian Nichols, are on the menu tonight," I replied with a devious smirk. His dick pulsed against my thigh. "Mmm. So, you *are* turned on?"

"Hell yeah."

My head buzzed, fueling my liquid courage and causing me to go a bit off script. "How often do you think about me?"

"More often than I should. More often than I've ever thought about any other woman in a long time," he admitted.

"And what do you think about when you think of me?" I asked, slowly gyrating against his dick.

"Mmm, shit. Everything... touching you, when's the next time I'm gon' run into you, shit, even being shot down by you."

I giggled. "Why being shot down?"

He bit down on his bottom lip before sliding his hands over my ass. "I like our banter. It's sexy to me."

I squinted my eyes. "Why do I feel like I can never take you seriously? You're always looking at me like you're undressing me with your eyes."

"Maybe I'm just reliving the past."

I paused. I thought I was nothing more than a drop in the bucket to him. All of a sudden, he had memories of me? "Well, a lot has changed in ten years."

"Mmm, I can see that."

"I would've done a lot of things differently back then had I been... more experienced."

"Differently like what?"

"Well, for instance, I would've had more foreplay. I would've kissed you more, savored the taste of your skin against my lips..."

He closed his eyes. "Mmm, what else?"

"I would've talked dirty to you," I answered, letting my bottom lip gently graze his earlobe.

"I like that shit."

I continued to gyrate my hips against him slowly. "How dirty would you have wanted me to get?"

"As dirty as you wanted," he growled, gripping my hips tighter.

The vibrations of his deep voice against my eardrum sent shivers down my spine. I licked my red-painted lips. "You sure you could've handled that back then?"

"Of course, and I can handle it now, too. That's for damn sure," he confirmed before flipping me over onto my back.

I smacked my palm against the side of his face with a hard *thwap* before shoving him off me. "I'm in charge tonight, remember?"

Jah remained on his back, holding his stinging jaw. "Damn, yo. My fault."

"Now, where do you want me to touch you?" I asked, circling his nipples with my fingertip.

"All over."

"Mmm," I said, resting my hand against the bulge in his jeans. "How hard are you right now?"

"I'm bricked up."

"You want me to sit on it and fuck you until I cum, or do you want me to make you beg for it?" I probed, running the back of my hand against his soft beard.

"You can ride this dick all fuckin' night, Jhordyn."

"Mmm. Good to know. Oh! Before I forget, I have something for you."

"Another surprise bigger than this?"

"Something like that," I replied before grabbing my clutch and slipping the cuffs out.

His eyes shifted between me and the silver cuffs in my hand. "You've used handcuffs before?"

I shrugged off his comment before glancing over my shoulder to see we'd gathered a bit of an audience. The viewers I so desperately craved turned me on as I locked his left wrist in a handcuff and attached the other side to the bedpost. I felt his arm tense up as he hesitated.

"Jho, I don't think we—"

"Shh." I silenced him with a quick kiss. "Don't worry about them. Just sit back and let me take care of you tonight. And if you're a good boy, I'll even suck your dick and let you bust in my mouth while all those people watch," I teased.

He bit his bottom lip. "Mmm, shit."

"Stop doing that shit."

"Doing what?"

"Biting your fucking lip like that."

"Why? Do you like it?"

"No. I love it. Now, let's see how hot we can get tonight, Mr. Fireman. But before we get to that, I want to play a game."

"What kind of game?" he quizzed.

"Never Have I Ever."

"What are the rules?"

"Hold up ten fingers. If I say something you've done, you strip, and vice versa."

"Okay, but you just locked up my wrist. How am I gonna strip?"

"Don't lose and you won't have to. But if you do lose, don't worry. I'll undress you nice and slow," I promised.

"Bet. You go first."

"Oh, I was *always* going first." I decided to start light with easy questions to get him warmed up. "Never have I ever slid into someone's DMs."

"Damn," he said with a chuckle, immediately putting down his first finger as I slid off his shoe. "Never have I ever invited anyone to a sex club to act out my sex fantasy."

I rolled my eyes before stepping out of my left heel. "Never have I ever had an intentional one-night stand."

He dropped a finger. "Never have I ever been catfished," he shot back.

"Me neither. Never have I ever slept with someone whose name I *didn't* know."

"Shit," he hissed, dropping another finger and allowing me to take off his other shoe and sock. "Fine. Okay. Never have I ever been in love."

My heart skittered. Of course, his ass had never been in love. He was a dog, and a dog with no master only loved itself. I hesitantly dropped a finger and stood without my heels. "Never have I ever used a cheap pickup line to meet a woman."

Jahtavian chuckled. "Damn. You got me losing out here," he replied, dropping a finger. I skipped over his other sock and leaned in to pull his shirt off, letting it hang around his left arm.

"You might as well quit while you're ahead and let me remove everything else. It's not like you came layered up," I teased.

"Nah, baby. I came to play. It ain't over until it's over. Let's go! Never have I ever used handcuffs or something similar in the bedroom." I pulled off my hot pants and let the fabric hit the floor before stepping out. Jahtavian looked me up and down, glancing at my black thong and bustier while licking his lips. "Never have I ever wanted you so fuckin' bad right now."

"Aht, aht!" I protested. "It wasn't your turn. It's mine."

"My fault."

"Never have I ever had a threesome."

Jah chewed his bottom lip before dropping another finger. I shot him a victorious smirk before unbuckling his pants and pulling them to his knees. I pulled them off, one leg at a time, before tossing them to the side.

"Never have I ever gone back to an ex," he stated.

I smirked before pulling off his other sock. "Haven't yet."

"Shit."

It was the moment I'd been waiting for. It was time to deliver my final blow and give the jackass the hee-haw he deserved. "Never have I ever had a summer romance, took someone's virginity, and then proceeded to fuck all her roommates."

# 7

## Love The Way You Lie

*"Hence the skillful fighter puts himself into a position which makes defeat impossible and does not miss the monument for defeating the enemy."*
*-Sun Tzu*

Jah's light expression shifted from humor to confusion. "Hold up. What?" he asked, brows dipping inward as his smile faded.

My hand slowly moved down his exposed chest to the lining of his boxer briefs—the last article of clothing he had on—where his dick stood at attention. "You heard me." I smirked at him before leaning in close. "Let me rephrase it for you. Never have I ever used a girl, fucked her friends behind her back, then threw her away like trash."

He shook his head. "Nah."

I sucked my teeth before stripping him of his briefs and giving the tip of his dick a tight squeeze. "Don't lie, Jah. It turns me off, and I'm *so* fucking wet right now."

I wanted nothing more but for Jahtavian to admit what he'd done—how he'd used women like me and gotten away with it time and time again without facing any consequences.

"All right. You're right. I was a complete dick to a lot of females in the past, especially you, Jhordyn." He complied as I gently stroked his long, thick shaft.

"Mmm. Tell me more."

"I was always too selfish to have a relationship, at least one with substance. It was all about pussy for me back then, but I-I'm different now."

I scoffed. "Oh, so now you believe in monogamy?"

"I'm pushing thirty. I want something different. And if it's still unclear, I want it with *you*."

I folded my arms across my chest. "So, you're saying you've evolved since college?"

"Of course, I have. Haven't you?"

"This isn't about me."

"Like hell it isn't. It's been about you since I saw you again. I wanna have all the things with you I've never had before. I want a second chance at a first impression witchu, Jhordyn, *and* your heart," he confessed as I stroked his dick.

I looked over my shoulder at the audience, then back at him. "We don't believe you, Jah. The audience and I want *real* emotion. I want you raw. Your pain is what I get off on," I whispered to him.

He didn't reply, so I stopped stroking him and snaked toward his chest, teasing and sucking his nipples before peppering kisses down his washboard abs. The more I kissed all over his body, the wetter I became. Torturing him with his own sexual need to release meant torture for me, too. I squirmed, watching him try to come up with ways to avoid admitting the *whole* truth.

"Shit, Jho," he groaned with pleasure. "What the fuck are you doing to me?"

I smirked. I liked making Jahtavian *want* what I was doing to him —making him want the punishment, the withholding of release. I stepped back to slide off my thong, then slid the wet fabric across his nose. "Tell me why I should let you have this sweet ass pussy again."

"I can show you far better than I can tell you, with one hand cuffed to the bedpost and all," he boasted before reaching out and grabbing me with his free hand.

Jahtavian's cat-like reflexes snagged at my wrist, reeling me toward him with one swift pull, landing me on top of him. He wasted no time landing his free hand between my sticky, wet thighs and right against my sweet spot. An unexpected moan slipped past my lips. I'd been trying to break him down, yet his virility still remained intact. I wanted him to beg my pussy for forgiveness all night long—beg to have me, *loudly*. Instead, he threw me off with the circular motion of his fingertips against my clit.

"I want to play a game now," he announced, gaining the unexpected upper hand.

My brows creased as I tried to regain control by grabbing his wrist while stifling another moan. "W-what?"

He slipped a finger inside me. "You heard me."

"What's this one?" I asked, melting under his experienced touch.

He grunted. "Damn, that pussy tight. Twenty-one questions."

I twisted my mouth to the side, teeth sinking into my bottom lip. "Any r-rules I s-should be a-aware of?" I stuttered, succumbing to the pleasure.

"Just answer the questions and try not to cum," Jahtavian replied as his thumb gently strummed my clit. "Have you ever fantasized about us while you were alone?" he inquired.

I mustered all the strength I had in me and pried myself away from his touch. "Fuck! You're not in control here!"

"Then let me see you touch it."

I smirked. "That's not a question."

"Am I the man you want to fulfill your sexual fantasy?"

"Who says I only have one?"

"Answer the first question."

"Maybe I do."

"Then I dare you to come show me."

Jahtavian had me dripping for him. I couldn't hide the lust behind my gaze, nor did I want to hold back any longer. I couldn't. Something in me snapped. I opened my purse and emptied its contents onto the bed, spilling out condoms, my flogger, and breath mints.

I ran my flogger forward and backward over his body, causing goosebumps to rise against his skin. The leather tassels traveled down his legs, up to his groin, and back up to his nipples before I repeated the same motion. Just when he started to relax, I smacked his thighs, leaving a delightful sting against his flesh. I found pleasure in watching his lower body squirm and his dick jump.

A soft moan escaped his lips. "Mmm, shit."

I straddled him, slicing my eyes right through him while biting my lip. I wanted my love juices to be his beard oil.

"You know what I think?" I asked, tilting my head to the side.

He shot me a naughty smile as if he was imagining all the things he was in store for. "What's that?"

"That you should lick me. I'm delicious," I stated before dropping the flogger and easing my pussy lips right onto his face.

I rocked back and forth against his soft lips as his long, experienced tongue explored my folds. Jahtavian's free hand gripped and smacked my ass. His aggression caused me to buck harder, faster, like a running hare.

I moaned while gripping my breasts. "Oooh shit. Fuck yeah. Lick that pussy just like that."

My eyes narrowed to half-mast as I focused on the heat and power radiating from my hips. The feathery strokes of Jahtavian's tongue were seconds away from making me cum.

I panted. "Ahhhh shit. Don't stop! Don't you dare fucking stop!"

I bucked faster in a frantic race to fulfillment, hellbent on experiencing the toe-curling sensation that awaited me. Soon, a passionate tide overtook me, and my body jerked and shook with fulfilment. It was the first time I'd felt fully alive. I climbed off his face and looked down at where I'd marked my territory. A smirk of satisfaction eased across my face as I eyed the sticky, wet sheen across his beard. My smile only widened when I saw his brick-hard dick. My dominant side only made him more rigid and engorged. I rolled a condom down his shaft before easing down on top of him, nice and slow.

"Ooooh shit," he growled as our heated flesh joined as one.

Jahtavian's fiery gaze blazed with lust as he bit down on his bottom lip. I rocked back and forth, fucking the tip of his dick for a few strokes before sliding down to the base. My fingertips gripped his chest, exploring the texture of his ripped muscles as the girth of his dick widened me with every rise and fall.

"Oh my God!" I screamed, nearly maddened with pleasure.

Jahtavian's hand smacked my ass, fueling my frenzy. I looked over my shoulder at the scant amount of people around us. Seeing their eyes on me as I took control made me even wetter. I bucked harder as Jahtavian's grip tightened around my waist, reddening my buttery brown skin. His husky voice moaning and whispering his need to release.

"Fuck, Jhordyn. This pussy is so fuckin' tight. I'm about to bust."

"Mmm, not yet, Mr. Fireman. Ladies first."

I leaned forward, lips landing on his. We shared a long, liquid kiss that pumped even more lust through me. He moaned in my mouth, tongue teasing my lips apart. Feeling my body molded to his after so long stirred up a primal need inside me that defied all rhyme and reason.

"Ooh, fuck! Fuck! I'm cumming, Jah!" I squealed as my body shook with pleasure on top of him.

He growled, smacking my bouncing ass with his free hand. "Ahh, shit. Yeah! Cum all over this dick, Jhordyn."

Jahtavian thrust his hips upward, stiffening his back as I

squealed. I panted, heart beating rapidly as I looked over my shoulder once more to see other couples fucking to the sight of us. One look at his curled toes, and I knew the sex had been mind-blowing for us both, but I refused to let him finish inside me—not even with a condom on. Instead, I eased myself off of him and jerked him off until he burst. Afterward, I didn't release him from his bond. I quickly grabbed my belongings and placed the keys to the cuffs on his panting chest before petting the top of his head and kissing his sweat-glazed forehead.

"Thanks for the ride."

# 8

## Take A Bow

*"Hence the saying: If you know the enemy and know yourself, your victory will not stand in doubt; if you know Heaven and know Earth, you may make your victory complete."*
*-Sun Tzu*

The sex club's pulse still hummed in my veins as I darted out of the door, heels clicking against the pavement. The night air was cool, carrying the faint aroma of a distant rain shower. My car, silver and sleek, awaited me in the lot—a private sanctuary to release the adrenaline rush behind having sex with Jah after so many years. I planned to head straight back to my grandmother's house to lay low and check in on the progress of the renovations.

The edges of the city were a different beast. The streets widened, and the amount of tall building clusters thinned out. I drove past gas stations and abandoned stores in strip malls, the asphalt unraveling like a black ribbon into the night. The night's chaos faded into my rearview, replaced by the drumming of my heartbeat. Finally, I pulled into the driveway of my house. It was a Victorian-style home under a canopy of tall, rooted oak trees. The exterior was charming with a wraparound porch, wooden rocker, and creaky porch swing. But it was the kitchen renovations that held my attention.

I stepped inside and slid off my heels before hurrying to the kitchen. I flipped on the switch to see that the renovations were almost complete, yet the space still wore the look of restoration. The old linoleum flooring had been ripped up and tossed, replaced with new, modern hardwood floors. The smell of fresh paint wafted off the soothing sage green walls, but patches of exposed brick still peeked out where my brand-new cabinets would be installed soon. The pendant lights above shone on the stripped countertops, awaiting their new quartz slabs. The new sink was in place, but the long-neck faucet had yet to be installed. I looked around with a smile. I couldn't wait to sit by the new kitchen nook and sip coffee while watching the sunrise.

Satisfied, I ascended the old wooden stairs to the second floor. The master bathroom was also nearing completion. The rehabbed shower was still missing its door and fixtures, and the new vanity mirror leaned against the wall yet to be installed, but I didn't mind. In a few more weeks, those imperfections would be distant memories. After a long shower in the guest bathroom, I slipped into the guest bed, burrowing under the fresh sheets. The room's walls were adorned with faded floral wallpaper and the scent of lavender from the plug-in by the nightstand permeated the room, soothing my tired body. As I closed my eyes, thoughts of my night with Jah danced through my head like sugarplum fairies. The night couldn't have gone more perfect. It was time to move on to the final phase of my plan: ghost his black ass.

---

*Two weeks later.*

I went Casper on his ass for two weeks, left his texts on read, ignored his calls, and didn't listen to his voicemails right away. I even temporarily hid his posts from my social media feeds just so I wouldn't be tempted to cyber sleuth what he'd been up to. Instead, I let the messages stack up like a game of Jenga. By the time I decided to pay him some attention and see what state of unrest my absence had put him in, I could read his distress and hear his undoing in his voice.

*"Yo, Jhordyn. It's me. What was that back at the club? That shit was wild, but I'm tryna see you again. Hit me up and let me know when we can link."*

*"I see you playing hard to get. I ain't seen you back at the apartment or nothing. Where you at? I told you, I ain't nothing like I used to be. For real, Jhordyn. I've been praying and working on myself. You're special."*

*"Where your ass at, Jhordyn? It's been over a week. You back with your imaginary boyfriend or something? I bet you his ass can't fuck you better than me. This dick is curved to your tight-ass walls, girl. Call me back."*

I snickered as I deleted them all one by one until I got to his latest message. *"Jhordyn, it's me. I'm for real about seeing you again. Why you ghosting me? Did I do something? Are you good? Hit me back so I know your ass ain't get kidnapped or–"* His voice cut out as the klaxon alarm sounded off in the background. *"Shit. I gotta go."*

The alarm ringing in the background and his abrupt hang-up made me tense. I looked at the date of the voicemail. He'd left it two days prior, and I hadn't received a call or text from him since.

"Shit," I mumbled, immediately regretting my schemes.

*What if he's dead, and I left him on read for weeks?* I checked his social media profiles, only to see he hadn't posted recently. I quickly searched the Houston news outlets for information on any recent fires. I clicked a recent news video titled *Three Injured as Houston Firefighters Battle Four-Alarm Fire*, and my stomach instantly knotted.

*"I'm Kirsten Shepard with Live Five News. I'm at the scene of a massive warehouse fire, as you can see from this huge bloom of smoke behind me. I'm told there are several firefighters from over four counties here responding to the fire and trying to knock down these flames.*

*"Houston's fire officials say that the fire occurred just before three o'clock this morning, where hundreds of wooden pallets went up in flames. We are not yet sure what spread the fire, but we do know that this started as a two alarm and has escalated to a four alarm fire because of a nearby diesel plant. Our team is also being told that three firefighters suffered minor injuries and have been transported to the local hospitals to be taken care of. The crews will be on scene throughout the night. Stick with Live Five News for more updates."*

As nervous as I was, my pride wouldn't let me call or text him back. I didn't know what to do. I wasn't his girlfriend, and I wouldn't be his neighbor for much longer. Hell, I was barely his friend to begin with. What would I look like popping up at every hospital asking questions about his health and safety like a lunatic?

I couldn't stop my thoughts from racing or my feet from pacing my new kitchen floor. Since I couldn't settle my nerves at home, I hopped in my car and drove back to the apartment, with secret hopes of running into him there. *Maybe he's not dead. Maybe he's just busy still fighting that fire.*

---

As I approached my front door, the light stench of decay wafted past my nose. Three separate bouquets of dead sunflowers lay wilted at my doorstep. Their once-fiery golden petals were brittle. I frowned, knowing exactly who they were from. Just as I bent down to pick up the limp floral remains, the door to Jahtavian's apartment creaked open. I straightened my posture, eyes narrowing on the woman who'd emerged, a melanated goddess with her coils pulled back into a low, neat bun. Her skin tone was the color of rich cocoa, and her big, brown eyes gleamed with mischief.

"Ah, so you're the owner of all the dead plants," the woman said, her voice holding a light chuckle.

"Guilty," I replied with a lighthearted shrug.

"Who's the poor schmuck that's all strung out over you?"

My heart raced. As curious as she was about me, I was willing to bet I was ten times more curious about her. She wasn't the girl he'd been dating when I planted the panties in his apartment. She wasn't posted on any of his social media profiles. So, who the fuck was she?

I cleared my throat. "That's a *long* story," I replied.

The mysterious woman chuckled, her lips curving upward into a good-humored smile. "I'm Carmen," she announced, extending her right hand.

"Jhordyn," I replied with a gentle handshake.

"Ah," she replied, assessing me from head to toe. "*You're* the new neighbor," she stated, musing for a few seconds. "Interesting."

I didn't like that she seemed to already know more about me than I did about her, and it took everything in me not to show it through my facial expressions. But I decided to play it cool even though the weight of curiosity rested on my shoulders like a cloak. "Are you one of the firefighters from Jahtavian's station?" I probed, keeping my tone light.

"No. I'm Jah's fiancée. I just came by to pick up some things to take back to the hospital."

My arm went limp, causing the wilted bouquets cradled in my grasp to hit the ground with a thud. The beating organ in my chest froze before bursting and ceasing to beat altogether. Somewhere amid my unraveling, I lost all feeling in my legs, and all I could hear was the ringing of an alarm in my ears. I didn't know if I'd been more thrown for a loop by the fact that Jahtavian was in the hospital or that it was his fiancée who'd broken the news to me.

"W–what did you say?" I stuttered as I bent down to pick up the flowers for the second time.

Carmen's airy giggle danced in the shared space between us. "Which part? Me being his fiancée or him being in the hospital?"

My cheeks burned as I tore my eyes to the floor before daring to land my gaze on her left hand. The diamond on her finger twinkled underneath the hallway lighting, and my stomach flopped before immediately souring. Sweat dripped down my spine, and my mouth pooled with fresh saliva. I wanted to avoid speaking out of fear that my voice would break or that I'd throw up everywhere, but I knew I had to say something.

"H-hospital? Is he okay?"

She dipped her chin with a nod. "Yeah. He should be discharged soon. Jah's quite the character, giving those nurses a run for their money in there. They'll probably be glad when he's gone. But I'll tell you just like I tell everyone else, he's mostly harmless."

I stood there, simmering with anger, yet trying not to show it. Smiling when all I really wanted to do was scream was such a nauseating feeling. "I'm sorry, but I have to go. T-Tell him to, uh, get well soon," I stammered before quickly jabbing the key into the lock and pushing inside before my smokescreen slipped.

"I will," she replied to my back as I sped through the door with my heart racing a million miles a minute. I didn't even bother turning back around to face her. I couldn't dare let her be an eyewitness to my unraveling.

The door slammed shut behind me, and my heart completely hardened as I bolted to the bathroom. After throwing up everything

I'd eaten for the day, I rinsed my mouth in the sink and looked up at my reflection. Over the last few weeks, I thought Jahtavian had become... *different*. I'd foolishly started to believe all that bullshit he'd spouted about growing up and wanting different things when all the while, he was still chocked full of shit. The moment I almost stopped questioning if he was serious, fate stepped in, and sucker punched my ass right in the gut.

I was pissed. No. I was more than pissed. I was *fucking livid*. Rage poisoned my veins. My apartment became the backdrop to my rollercoaster of emotions. The lifeless sunflowers lay tossed, forgotten near the front door as I tore through my bedroom. My anger became a wildfire consuming everything of value—my sanity, my reason. I had half a mind to follow her to the hospital just so I could confront him and blow up his life myself. But instead, I decided to take my rage out alone. I barreled down the hallway, stomping with every step. The kitchen drawers shook as I yanked them open and shook out everything inside, exposing the empty lining underneath. The framed photo of my grandmother and me from my sixteenth birthday, our beaming grins frozen in time, shattered against the floor.

"Fuck!" I screamed, my voice raw with emotion. "Why? Why the fuck did I fall for him again?"

The memories flooded back, each more painful than the last. I wished there was a delete button inside my brain that could permanently erase the day we met and every other existence of him from my memory. I'd seen a softer side of him, one I never knew existed. But with Carmen's revelation, his entire "reformed good guy" façade shattered like shards of glass. Jahtavian was a wolf who'd been wrapped in sheep's clothing for so long he'd actually convinced himself and everyone around him that he was one of them. I was the only one who seemed to know the truth.

Tears blurred my vision as I stormed back down the hall to my room and ripped open the closet door. I flung my accessories and hanging clothes into the air, including the delicate pearls my grandmother had given me for my baptism when I was eleven. I hurled the strand of silken pearls against the wall, watching the chain pop and the pearls roll in a million different directions. I sank to the floor, my tantrum giving way to misery.

I'd been a motherfucking fool, chasing revenge and the ghosts from my past, naively thinking that I was in the driver's seat. When in reality, Jahtavian Nichols had been nothing more than a puppet master pulling my strings. I sniffled as I looked around. It took all that for me to see that he wasn't worth it. He never had been. The wreckage of my apartment would stand as my witness. It was time for me to officially unplug from the matrix, lick my wounds, and move the fuck on for good.

I wiped my tears with the back of my hand. "Well played, Jahtavian. Well fucking played," I muttered.

# 9

## n-Break My Back

*Three weeks later.*

*"In battle, there are not more than two methods of attack– the direct and the indirect; yet these two in combination give rise to an endless series of maneuvers."*
*-Sun Tzu*

The weeks flew by, and somehow, Cupid still had his foot up my ass with a size eleven shoe. I was sadder than sad. It was like déjà vu, circa my sophomore year all over again. So, I did what any woman would do: I threw myself into my work to try to block out as much pain as I could. I sat in the lab, eyes glazed over as I stared at my computer screen trying to document reports and update patient medical records. I was clad in my white lab coat with my hair pulled back into a low, neat bun. I needed to focus on work, but I couldn't. I could barely concentrate on anything for long stints of time, and in my line of work, that wasn't acceptable. I still thought about Jahtavian nonstop. I didn't know how I could even miss him knowing what I knew, but I did. I even started to consider the possibility that I'd fallen in love with his ass. And not that summer love I'd felt all those years ago. The feelings eating away at my heart were different the second time around. I'd gotten what I wanted. I'd won. I should've been smiling, right? But I couldn't.

My thoughts were transferred to my vibrating phone. I flipped it over to see the name of the moving company I'd hired across the screen and quickly pressed accept.

"Hello?"

"Hi. Is this Jhordyn Davis?"

"Yes. This is she."

"Hi. This is John from Zip's Movers. I'm just calling to confirm your move-in date. We're all set to transfer your belongings from your apartment to your house this Thursday."

I nodded. "Yes. That's correct."

My heart skipped a beat just thinking about the apartment. I couldn't stand the thought of running into Jahtavian. As hurt as I was, I'd gone cold turkey on all things Jah—blocked his number, deleted my Finsta account, and shredded the existence of my carefully curated revenge timeline—all in the name of heartbreak.

---

I DROVE MY CAR DOWN MY FAMILIAR STREET, AND MY MIND WAS already planning the rest of my night—dinner, shower, and binge-watching reality TV to make me forget about my own drama and focus on someone else's. As I rounded the corner, I was met with an unexpected sight. A row of fire trucks blocked the road with blinking red lights. My heart beat double time inside my chest. *What's going on? Oh my God! What if there's a fire?* I shifted the car into park near the curb and approached the first firefighter I saw with the last name Jackson on the back of his uniform.

"E-excuse me. I live on this street. Can you tell me what happened here?"

"Hi. Yes, ma'am. We received a few reports of a gas leak at the house just down the street. We've got our guys investigating now, but for safety reasons, no one can enter the area until we've given the all-clear," he explained.

Panic swelled inside me like a balloon. "Which house?"

"Twelve-Ninety-Two Holland Lane."

My breaths slightly eased. My house was right in the danger zone, two houses down, but I was thankful it wasn't the source of the leak or going up in smoke.

"We're doing our best to work as quickly as we can. But until we're sure, you'll have to clear the area for now."

"Can I stay in my car? I'm parked right back there," I informed him.

"Yes, ma'am. That's fine."

"Thanks."

I nodded just as the realization hit me. The unexpected gas leak spelled takeout for dinner, a pause on the hot shower, and trading up reality TV for YouTube videos on my phone while I waited for them to give the all-clear. I glanced back at my running car, where the grocery bags sat in the back seat, my pint of cookies and cream ice cream thawing by the second.

"Shit," I mumbled.

As I twisted on my heels to head back to my car, I heard a familiar voice call my name. "Jho?"

I froze. *No. No. It cannot be him.*

My heart thumped as I slowly turned toward the familiar voice. There, in his firefighter turnouts, stood Jah looking ruggedly handsome. We both looked shocked to see each other. Our eyes locked, and time seemed to stretch like taffy.

"Jhordyn? W-what are you doing here?" he stammered.

"I moved," I answered in an icy tone. "And I don't want to talk to you."

His brows dipped with confusion as he massaged his sweaty forehead. It was as if he was trying to make sense of my words. "Yo, I've been trying to reach you for weeks. Why didn't you—"

I waved my hand before cutting him off. "I don't understand why you're still talking to me."

I turned away from him. It took everything in me not to stomp against the pavement like a child having a temper tantrum. Jahtavian followed, desperation in his tone. "Jho, please—"

I'd had enough of our surprise reunion. I reached my car, slammed the door shut, and cranked up the music. The bass vibrated through the car speakers, successfully drowning him out. He stood there, helplessly watching me. *If only the music could visually block him out, too.* The lyrics to Moneybagg Yo's "Toxic" merged with my annoyance, enveloping me. *Not today, Satan. Not ever again.*

He stepped back before yanking open the driver's side door. In all my rage, I'd forgotten to lock myself inside. My hands trembled as I gripped the steering wheel. Jah stood there, his brooding expression a mix of confusion and annoyance. "I'm not playing games with you, Jhordyn, and I'm not leaving until you explain yourself!"

I snapped my neck at him while creasing my forehead. "Explain myself? What the hell do I need to explain to you?"

His mouth set in a hard line before he spoke. "Because you fuckin' ghosted me, yo!"

"You want an explanation?" I snapped, raising my voice as I balled my fists. "Fine! I met your precious little fiancée, Jahtavian! Carmen! She was at your apartment, and we had a nice little chat." Jahtavian blinked before opening his mouth to speak, but I wasn't finished. "And before you fix your fuckin' lips to lie, I don't care! I don't care about your explanations or your weak ass excuses. I'm done! I'm done, and I'm good! Okay? So just go back and do your fucking job so I can get inside my house before it gets dark!" I barked.

His eyes widened. "Jhordyn, listen. It's not what you think. Carmen is my homegirl from Station Twenty-Two. We graduated the fire academy together. I had her come by and pick up things from my apartment while I was in the hospital."

"Didn't I say I didn't fucking care?"

"That's not my girlfriend, and she's damn sure not my fiancée. We're just friends. I swear to you it's not like that."

I tightly pinned my arms against my chest. "Then what the fuck is it like then, Jah? Huh? Because I can't tell the difference between the version of you in college and the version standing in front of me now. Talking all that shit about you changed when ain't a goddamn thing different or special about your black ass. You still the same toxic ass nigga!" I barked, knowing my mouth may have survived another round with him, but my heart wouldn't.

He shot a silencing glare at me before biting back. "You finished, or you done?"

I leaned back, my brows raised at the hardening of his tone. "Excuse me?"

"You got your fuckin' mind so made up about me that you only hear and see what you want! She told me she met you. She thought you were a random female. So, yeah, it's something we do to keep bitches at bay. Carmen's a lesbian who's engaged to a *woman*, not me. Look at her social media. I swear to you, Jhordyn. I promise you I'm not on no bullshit. If I had my phone right now, I'd call her on FaceTime and let her tell you herself."

His words did nothing but make my head spin in circles. That's all Jahtavian and I seemed to be good for. Either he was the one playing games, or I was.

I swung my head in a no. "You can call Carmen on FaceTime or whatever. I don't care! I can't do this shit with you anymore. I won't! I've already got fucking PTSD," I said, shaking my head. "No. I'm done, Jahtavian. I got what I wanted, and I'm done. I don't need the drama."

Sadness clouded his features. "What? What do you mean you got what you wanted?"

Before I could respond, I heard an update come in over his walkie-talkie. *"The area has been cleared. Let the civilians know they can re-enter their homes."*

"Looks like you've gotta go, and so do I," I answered before slamming my car door shut and putting the car in drive.

---

I stirred on the couch at the sound of the doorbell. My eyes popped open to see the soft glow from the TV looking back at me. I sat up disoriented just as the doorbell rang again, jolting me fully awake.

"Who the hell?" I mumbled.

I reached for my phone to check the time. It was half past midnight. My heart drummed as I tiptoed to the hallway closet to retrieve a baseball bat before creeping toward the front door. The floor creaked underneath each step. I looked through the peephole, and my breath caught in my throat. It was Jahtavian—tall, rugged, and wearing his blue firefighter uniform.

I unlocked both locks before cracking open the door. "Jahtavian? What the hell are you doing here so late?"

"My shift just ended, and I want to finish our conversation from earlier. Please, Jhordyn," he begged, his vulnerability raw under the moonlight.

His dark-eyed gaze tugged at my heart strings, but I refused to fold. My anger flared through my nostrils. It had taken me hours and half a bottle of wine to forget our last interaction. One look at him, and I was ready to rip his head off all over again.

I swung my head in a sharp no. "There's nothing more to talk about. I said all I had to say earlier. Besides, it's late. The only things open right now are legs and Waffle House. Take your ass home!"

I tried to slam the door in his face, but his boot blocked it. His sorrowful brown eyes pleaded with me. "Jhordyn, listen. It's not what you think. Carmen—she's just my friend. Please—"

My grip tightened on the baseball bat. "Stop insulting my intelligence! I don't want to hear your lame ass excuses. You left me broken, Jah. *Again*! Now leave before I—"

He cut me off by pushing inside and sweeping me off my bare feet. My grip on the bat released as Jahtavian tossed me over his shoulder and marched up the stairs.

"What the hell are you doing?"

"Which bedroom is yours?"

"Jahtavian, put me down!" I protested, slapping his back.

"Which bedroom is yours, Jhordyn? I won't ask your ass again!" he barked with a twinge of anger laced in his voice.

"I'm sleeping in the guest room. First room on the left."

He kicked open the bedroom door and tossed me onto the bed. I quickly sat up on my elbows and scooted back against the iron-wrought headboard. Jahtavian gripped my wrist before pulling a pair of handcuffs from his back pocket.

My breath hitched. "Are those—"

"Shut the *fuck* up, Jhordyn," he grumbled, tightening the cuff around my wrist. "I'm in control right now. You hear me? You're going to listen to me fully. Every time your ass interrupts me, I'm going to strip you of something."

My lips twisted in a sick grin when he clinked the other end of the cuffs to my headboard. *Now he's getting the idea.* Toying with Jahtavian's heart may have all been a part of my revenge game, but I wasn't lying when I said my tastes were on the spicier side. I liked being the dominant one *and* being submissive. The question was, could he do it?

"Jah, I–"

He drew in a frustrated breath. "Oh, so you thought I was fuckin' playing?" he growled, ripping off my sweatpants.

I licked my lips before twisting my free hand over my mouth to emulate a lock and key. Jahtavian smirked at me before pulling out his phone, ready to prove his innocence. "She's engaged to someone else. Look at her social media. I swear—"

"I don't care about her damn social media. You hurt me, Jah!" I blurted out, completely forgetting to keep quiet.

He wagged his head before slowly sliding down my panties. As much as I didn't want to look at his phone, curiosity tugged at me. I hesitated, torn between my anger and curiosity. I shot a quick glance at the bright screen. My heart pounded. Carmen's social media—a glimpse into the life of the woman he claimed was *just* his homegirl.

"Show me," I answered, softly submitting.

Instead of pulling off my shirt, Jahtavian swiped through her photos individually. There was Carmen, radiant, but not with him. With someone else, just as he'd said. "She's engaged to Alexia. Jho, I swear—I know flashing the ring and playing was tasteless on her part, but she felt bad once I told her how I felt about you."

The truth hung heavy in the air like a dark cloud. My anger wavered as he spoke up again. "And I get why you doubted me. You made me realize some harsh truths about myself. I was a dick to you back in college, but I'm for real when I say I'm done with that life. I'm a man who knows what and *who* I want."

"You broke me... I didn't think a thing like that could happen twice."

Jahtavian reached for my free hand. "Then let me fix you."

"Do it. Take what you want... if you can."

Jahtavian took my words for what they were, a challenge. He pounced on me, his lips attaching to mine as I hooked my free arm around his neck. The longer we kissed, the more hot and bothered we became. Jahtavian's fingertips danced across my buttery brown skin like a familiar tune, taking wild and fierce possession of my body.

His touch sent warmth cascading through my chest. My hormones percolated as my nipples hardened, beckoning to be sucked.

His hands eased up my shirt, stopping just before he cupped my breasts. "Where's your bag of tricks?"

My eyes darted over toward the nightstand before shifting back toward him. He pulled open the drawer and grabbed my flogger. The leather tassels tickled the inside of my naked thighs before sliding up and down my sweet spot.

I bit down on my bottom lip. "Mmm."

"You like that shit?" he asked before angrily feasting on my neck.

"Mmhmm."

He jerked his head toward me. "I didn't hear you."

"Yes!"

His hands, strong and gentle, mapped out every curve and crevice of my body. My eyes slid closed just as I felt the tender assault of my nipples with his tongue. He tugged at my nipples with his teeth, showing no mercy to my sensitive flesh. My mouth gaped open to an O-shape as I palmed the back of his head and tilted mine back in ecstasy. The more pain I endured, the more turned on I became. He ran his hands through my hair, sniffing it before smacking my breasts.

"Oooh shit, yeah."

Jahtavian kissed me before running his thumb down my bottom lip and chin. He circled my diamond-hard nipples with his index finger. The tables had turned, and this time, he was the one denying and teasing me until I begged for release.

I moaned. "Mmm."

A wanting ache washed over me as he pried open my moistened clench. My clit was already swollen with anticipation. I squirmed under his touch, feeling his fingertips poised at my slit. Jahtavian gripped my throat as he finger fucked me until I creamed, leaving his fingers white. His hands spoke to my body in a language only they could understand. He withdrew his fingers, leaving me dripping and begging for more. The feeling of him was so addictive that I couldn't control myself.

My chest was aflame with passion—an attraction that became

something much more dangerous than lust. He pulled my head backward, and my lips parted in desire as I waited for his words, his touch, his control. I was aching to cum all over his dick. Instead of speaking, he leaned in, kissing me hard so I knew how badly he wanted me. I felt his tongue at the back of my throat as his greedy mouth took bold possession of mine.

He pulled away only to undress. Jahtavian was a handsome, hypnotic, and powerful creature. His body was a beautiful landscape of tight abs, solidly carved thighs, and a hell of a package between his thighs. He stood before me, naked and erect, as he stroked the tip of his dick in a slow, repetitive rhythm, watching me squirm with anticipation.

"You want this dick?"

"Mmhm."

"You wanna cum all over it, don't you?"

I wilted as my breaths quickened. "Oooh, yes."

"Not yet. I wanna stretch that pussy out before I fuck you," he said forcefully.

For years, I'd prayed for a man who could see the fire behind my eyes and not be afraid to play with it.

"Say what you want to do to me, and I'll let you," I replied unapologetically. It was my final surrender.

The side of his lips lifted in a satisfying smirk. "I wanna slide my tongue around you like a snake and make you mine with every scream. I wanna watch you play with your pussy while I fuck you with a finger in your ass. I wanna flip you over and bite that perfect, round ass of yours like the sweet peach I know it is. Simply put, I want you at my mercy tonight, Jhordyn."

Jahtavian made it clear he wanted me to burn, tremble, and yearn for him. And the worst part of it all? I wanted to. He went back into my nightstand drawer and pulled out my dildo and rose vibrator. Then, he unhooked the cuff from the headboard and snapped it around my other wrist, binding them together. He grasped my knees and eased them apart, focused totally on me.

"Close your eyes and tilt your head back while you play with your pussy," he instructed.

My lids lowered, and I felt him trace the shape of my body's peaks and valleys before turning on the vibrator and putting it in my hand. His hand covered mine, placing the toy against my clit. My body shook and jerked upon contact as the toy sucked my sweet spot. I bucked forward, hunching the vibrator like a dog in heat.

"Oooh shit! Shit! Shit! That feels so fucking good." I panted.

But the pleasure didn't stop there. Jahtavian dove between my thighs, laying sweet kisses all over the lower half of my body before inching the seven-inch dildo inside me. My breath hitched at the double sensation. He licked the inner face of my smooth thighs before slipping a finger into my asshole, devastating my control. There were parts of me that had been completely untouched by another soul until he came along. His brazen hands breached my every defense, leaving his mark on every single inch of me. The double penetration and the clit sucking sent me into a frenzy.

"Ooooh fuckkkkkkkk! Yes! Yes! Yes! I'm cummminnggggg!" I screamed as I came harder than I'd ever cum in my life. It was a release I'd never experienced, but I was eager to sample again.

He slid the toy out of me and kissed my clit. "Mmm, look at that pretty pussy glistening," his dirty, gravelly words uttered against my flesh.

The aftershocks of pleasure washed over me, causing my body to tick and jerk without my control. "I'm ready now. Please, Jah," I pleaded, my eyes drunk with pleasure and stationed on him.

He shook his head. "You don't want me to make love to you. You want me to fuck you. You want me to take that pussy because it's always been mine. Hasn't it? You love being chased and submissive. You wanna be a slut for me. So come on, Jhordyn. Get on those knees and show me how dirty you can get."

He'd commanded me in such an insanely dominant way that I followed his authority instantly. I scooted off the bed and dropped to my knees. He smacked my ass and gripped the back of my head.

"You wanna suck this dick, don't you?"

I slowly nodded, mesmerized by the way he stroked his dick. I bit my lip at the sight of pre-cum pooling from the tip. He stepped forward, and I opened my mouth, creating the perfect wet, warm opening for his dick to land in. I gripped his shaft, stroking it while I licked and sucked the head.

"That's a good fuckin' girl. Suck all the pre-cum off that dick."

His dominant commands made me even wetter, which was something I didn't even know was possible. He spread his fingers wide over the crown of my head, fingertips gripping my textured roots. Jah continued fucking my mouth and calling me a good girl through his moans. I'd never technically sucked a real dick before; I only practiced in private with my dildos. So, hearing his moans was like music to my virgin dick-sucking ears. Hearing Jahtavian moan was one of the sexiest sounds ever.

"Ahhhh shit," he hissed, gritting his teeth for control before pulling me back to my feet.

The moment I'd been waiting for had arrived. He bent me over the bed and smacked my ass before pushing inside me from behind. We both released pleasing moans as he gripped my nape.

Heat burned my cheeks. "Oooh fuck! It feels soooo good!" I squealed, poking my ass out for him.

"You're mine, now—only mine. Understood?" he growled into my ear.

I nodded. I'd finally found someone who seemingly respected, adored, and dominated me. In return, I would bow, yield, submit, and succumb to him. He fucked me hard, wanting me sore and raw the next day. As if I'd ever be able to forget.

Jah gripped my waist as tears of pleasure streamed down my face. "Oooh, yes! Yes!" I cried, rubbing my clit in fast circles. I bucked back against him, fucking like I'd never fucked before. My body, lips, and my pussy had all been possessed by him. His hands smacked and gripped my bouncing flesh before he pulled out of me and flipped me onto my back. He held my gaze as his fingertips tilted my chin upward so that my eyes were trained on his.

"This pussy is mine," he whispered, voice thick with lust.

"Always has been." I breathed, barely able to utter words.

I felt boneless, pinned underneath him like a human pretzel bending to his will. Yet, I'd never felt such pleasure, such desire. It was as if all my anger and resentment had been balled up and turned into pure lust. His fingertips tightened around my throat as he dipped back inside me, delivering strokes with the essential speed and precision to make me cum back to back. He had me screaming to the rooftops each time a new wave of uncontrollable pleasure washed over me.

"Holy fucking shit! Oh my God! Oh my God! I don't think I can take any more!" I yelped.

I saw the delight in his eyes as he placed his hand over my mouth to muffle my moans before flipping me on top of him.

"Mmm, fuck," he growled, sliding his thumb into my mouth for me to suck on.

I absorbed the feel of his dick before bouncing up and down on him with my wrists still bound together. My breasts bounced up and down as I leaned forward, holding onto his muscles while he thrust his hips upward. I rocked forward, winding my hips while he massaged my clit. His fingertips edged me closer to my next climax. I'd cum so many times I'd lost count of the official number.

# 10

## Reversal of the Dog

*"In war, then, let your great object be victory, not lengthy campaigns."*
*-Sun Tzu*

Jahtavian and I went for rounds of dirty, sexy, passionate sex until the sun peeked over the horizon. The euphoric aftermath was damn potent. I smiled when I rolled over and saw the first few rays of sunlight stretching across the sky—delicate hues of pink and orange. We lay side by side, cocooned between my soft, sex-worn sheets, our fingers gently laced. The air smelled of sex and the promise of something new. My eyes pinged from the dove-gray walls down to the crumpled indigo duvet at the foot of the bed as the sunlight spilled in through the large window to the room's right.

My velvety legs intertwined with his as I nestled my wild head of hair against Jah's broad, tattooed chest. His heartbeat was steady, the rhythm matching his chest's relaxed rise and fall. I smiled as his fingertips traced circles on my bare arm, savoring the warmth of his delicate touch.

Jahtavian shifted, propping himself up on his elbows before looking at me. His eyes crinkled at the corners as he gazed into my eyes. "I got a question."

"What?"

"What did you mean yesterday when you said you got what you wanted?"

There was an uptick in my heartbeat. I blushed, feeling the warmth of embarrassment spread from my cheeks down to my chest. My thoughts raced a million miles a second. *Shit. This is it. The moment I've been dreading. How do I tell him the truth without him thinking I'm crazy? Do I spill my secret and risk losing him, or do I lie to cover my tracks and risk losing him anyway? Do I even want him?*

"This is all going to sound crazy," I stated with a long sigh.

"After all the nasty shit we just did? You can say whatever you gotta say to me."

I cleared my throat, knowing I had to come clean. "You broke my heart back in college. You took my virginity and then fucked all my roommates. Then I lost my grandmother after everything went south with us, and when I reached out to you about it, you blocked me. That really left me shattered, Jah. As badly as I wanted to let it go, or as much as I told myself you weren't worth the trouble, I couldn't. I vowed to make you pay for what you did. I wanted to break your heart like you did mine."

His brow furrowed. "What do you mean?"

"When I found out we were in the same city again, I started plotting how to get my revenge. I followed you online through a Finsta account. When I saw that you moved, I decided to do the craziest thing I've ever done in my entire life and moved in next door."

"Hold up. You moved into my building on purpose?"

I nodded as the weight of my confession hung over me like a dark cloud. "It was more than that. It was all orchestrated. I wanted you to feel everything I felt when you played in my face and walked away so easily. So, I planted the panties in your apartment. I played hard to get by pretending to have a man.

"I wanted you to want me, Jah. I wanted you to chase me so that I could toy with your heart. It was all fun and games until I listened to your voicemails and found out about the fire. That's when I started to feel weird about it all. I guess I just got so caught up in playing the game, you know? It was addictive. I was invisible to you for so long that it felt good to be noticed—to be desired knowing I was the one pulling the strings the entire time. It was twisted as hell, I know. But in some way, revenge was my shield to protect my heart from you or anybody else."

"I mean, I can't lie. This shit does sound crazy. I get that I fucked up back then, but you've had to have dated other guys after me, right? I mean, why go through all this trouble for just me?"

I fell silent for a few fleeting seconds. "Have I talked to guys and gone out on dates? Of course. Have I ever gone further than first base with anyone other than you? No. I thought losing my virginity would be no big deal, but I was angry and broken when things ended like they did. I couldn't risk giving that part of myself away to a man again."

"Hold up. Have you been with anybody but me?"

"Do my variety of sex toys count?"

His chest deflated with a hard sigh. "Shit. Jhordyn, I know I've said this shit a million times at this point, but I'm sorry for what I did to you back then. If I'm being honest, out of all the girls I messed with back then or fucked over, you were my biggest regret."

"Seriously?"

"Yeah. It's not like I thought about you every day or anything but seeing you again after so long held a mirror up to my face that I couldn't look away from. But this, us, it's real now. I really do care about you."

His response was a mix of surprise and compassion. Instead of judging me for what I'd done, he acknowledged my pain and the part he played in it. "Does this mean you forgive me?" I inquired.

The room was hushed. I felt a whirlwind of emotions as I waited for his response. My heart galloped with vulnerability, fear, and a mustard seed of hope. Could forgiveness triumph over unhealed wounds and vengeful schemes? Would Jah's forgiveness and willingness to put our pasts in our rearview pave the way for a second chance at something real between us—a chance to rewrite our history?

Jahtavian reached for my trembling hand, pulling it to his lips and pressing a kiss to my knuckles. "Neither of us can change the past, but we can dictate our future."

A mix of relief and uncertainty fluttered inside me as my brows raised toward my hairline. My heart twittered in my chest. Unbeknownst to him, Jahtavian's apology and words of forgiveness pulled me from the depths of my past pain. "You seriously want a future with me after everything I told you?"

"I want you. And if you ask me, I think you did all that wild shit because you love me," he said with a smirk as he brushed his thumb against my cheek.

My brows heightened. "What do *you,* of all people, know about love?"

"That's the thing, I don't know shit. I've never been in love before. But I *never* miss anyone, and I missed the hell out of you, Jhordyn. Back in college, I said and did a lot of shit I didn't believe in or knew was wrong, all in the name of pussy and being young and reckless. And I'm trying hard to show you this isn't a game or a phase. I'm done with that shit. You're the one I want to have my first monogamous relationship with."

"That's the problem. I missed you too. I didn't plan on falling for you like this again. But I did, and now, I'm torn. I'm not sure I'm ready for romance. If it's just sex that you want, I can handle that. What I can't handle is fully opening up my heart to you and things going left. The first time I did it, it fucked with me for so many years I went a little cuckoo."

Jah's smile was tender. "I want you and only you, and I promise, I mean it this time."

I studied his expression, seeing a level of seriousness in his eyes I'd never seen before. Call me crazy, but a look that made the hairs on my skin rise? That couldn't be faked. *I think he means it.* I wrapped my arms around his neck and kissed him, feeling a calming wave of assurance wash over me. He wasn't the same guy I'd once had a crush on or the one I'd plotted revenge against. And neither was I. The woman who made Jahtavian Nichols surrender his heart had surrendered hers, too.

# Epilogue

**hat Lovers Do**

*One year later.*

*"Anger may in time change to gladness; vexation may be succeeded by content."*

*-Sun Tzu*

"*Summer rain whispers me to sleep and wakes me up again*," Jah sang loudly over the sound of the running shower upstairs.

I hummed along softly to "Summer Rain" by Carl Thomas blasting through the bathroom speaker as I moved about the kitchen, the fresh hardwood floors gleaming under my bare feet. The sun streamed through the large bay window on the back of the house where my potted herb plants sat. I'd woken up alongside Jah with his six o'clock alarm to make us breakfast before work.

The coffee machine rippled, filling the space with its rich hazelnut aroma and waking me up with each deep inhale. I pushed up the sleeves on Jah's oversized Houston FD sweatshirt before cracking a few eggs into a mixing bowl and whisking them with milk to make them fluffy. The sizzle of butter in the frying pan made me think of my grandmother, which instantly brought a smile to my face. I was determined to scramble the eggs just how he liked them—with a sprinkle of fresh oregano from the windowsill.

As the eggs cooked, my mind wandered. It was funny how Cupid could sneak up on you when you least expected it, running down on your heart like a drive-by at a red light. Falling in love was like ripping your heart out of your chest, throwing it out of a moving plane, and hoping the other person would catch it. And yet, I'd never been happier. Never in a million years did I think Jahtavian Nichols and I would be building a life together, but I guess even my mind could be changed.

We'd officially been together for a few months shy of a year and couldn't have been happier together. I'd flown with him to meet his parents in Florida, and he'd met mine over Sunday dinner in my backyard when they drove up from Waco. Of course, his charming ass won them over on the first try. We'd even gone on double dates with Carmen and her wife, Alexia. Aside from our sexy sleepovers, I enjoyed my space and alone time. We kept our living arrangements separate since he worked twenty-four-hour shifts three days a week.

The two pieces of whole-grain toast popped out of the toaster, returning me to the present. I finished cooking the eggs and slicing a fresh avocado before plating the avocado toast and eggs on the table, waiting for him. The shower upstairs turned off, and I knew it was only a matter of time before he came dressed in his blue uniform shirt and pants. I swiped up a few loose strands of hair that had fallen from my messy bun before pouring the coffee into two mugs. Soon after, Jah descended the stairs and appeared in the kitchen. His bare chest was damp with water droplets as his towel hugged his waist below his

V-cut. I remained upright at the counter, heart skipping beats as a smirk appeared on my face.

"Morning," I greeted him, my eyes crinkling at the corners. "Why aren't you dressed for work?"

He crossed the room in wide steps, snaking his arms around my waist as he leaned in to kiss the side of my neck. "Mmm. Good morning, beautiful. What's all this?"

I leaned into his embrace, drawing in a deep breath as I felt the familiar warmth of his skin. "I made us breakfast."

He stole a quick kiss before reaching for the steaming coffee mug, taking a sip, and setting it back down. "Mmm. It looks good, but, uh, what if I told you I had a taste for something different this morning?" he quizzed.

I grinned. "Is that right?"

"Mmhm. Yeah."

"What exactly did you have in mind?"

He picked me up and placed me on the sunlit countertop before stealing another kiss. His lips were soft and attentive, igniting a wildfire inside me. I gently sucked on his bottom lip, tasting the remnants of hazelnut coffee on his lips and the promise of something long-term —a connection deeper than lust. Jahtavian wasted no time pulling his sweatshirt over my head and peppering kisses all over my collarbone and breasts before inching down my sweet spot. My hands found his waist and toyed with the lining of his towel, loosening it with a single tug.

As I sat there, staring into Jahtavian's eyes, I couldn't help but reflect on how deeply I'd fallen for him. I wondered if he knew how much he meant to me. How his existence filled the vacant holes in my life, how his anxiety-filled firefighting stories had become the soundtrack to my days. I wanted to tell him. Hell, I wanted to shout it from the rafters some days, but maybe some things were better left unsaid. Instead, I opted for a more straightforward approach.

I traced the curve of his bearded jaw. "I love you."

"I love you, too."

The End

# Afterword

**A note from K.L. Hall.**

Reader,

Thank you for reading *T.A.N.* (*Toxic A*s N***a*): *An Erotic Novella*. If you've made it this far, I hope you'll consider telling me what you thought about the book in the form of a **five-star review and/or rating**. Don't hesitate to let me know what you'd like to see from me next! I thoroughly enjoy reading your thoughts and hearing from you as well! I'm always striving to attract new readers and retain current ones, and reviews are one of the easiest ways to attract readers. If you loved the book, tell a friend, and most importantly, let me know!

All my love,
K.L. Hall

# About the Author

K.L. Hall is a national bestselling and award-winning author. As a serial storyteller, Hall has penned over three dozen titles in various genres—including African American urban fiction and romance, paranormal, children's books (as Kimberley M.), and non-fiction. Her fictional stories straddle the intersection of classic Urban and spellbinding Romance.

**Highly Acclaimed Titles:**

In the Arms of a Savage: (Peaked at #1 in Women's Fiction)

The Potomac Falls Series (Peaked at #1 and #2 in African American Erotica)

Sign up for my mailing list to stay updated with new releases, giveaways, sneak peeks, and more! Click this link: https://bit.ly/38RMpV5

**Connect with me on social media:**

Facebook: https://www.facebook.com/authorklhall

Twitter: https://twitter.com/authorklhall

Instagram: https://www.instagram.com/officialklhall/

Website: https://www.authorklhall.com

**Other novels by K.L. Hall:**

Diary of a Hood Princess 1-3

Rise of a Street King: The Justice Silva Story (*Spin-Off to the Diary of a Hood Princess series*)

Broken Condoms and Promises 1-3

In the Arms of a Savage 1-3

Built for a Savage: Blaze and Camille's Love Story (*Spin-Off to the In the Arms of a Savage Series*)

A Ruthle$$ Love Story 1-3

Fallin' for the Alpha of the Streets 1-2

The Most Savage of Them All: The Wolfe Calloway Story (*Prequel to the In the Arms of a Savage Series*)

When a Gangsta Loves a Good Girl

Caught Between My Husband and a Hustler

The Illest Taboo 1-2

To the Only Thug I'll Ever Love

A Lover's Heist: Chief and Gianna's Love Story

A Lover's Heist II: Rome and Lira's Love Story

A Lover's Heist III: Baby and Skai's Love Story

Crushed Velvet & Cashmere

Crushed Velvet & Cashmere 2

Entanglements

Never Had a Bad Boy Love Me So Good

Good Girls Always Got a Thing for the Thugs

Professor Zaddy: A Potomac Falls Novel

Bound in the Arms of a Thug: Chop & Kendyl's Love Story

**Short Reads + Novellas:**

Bi-Curious: An Erotic Tale

Bi-Curious 2: Tastes Like Candy

A Savage Calloway Christmas (*Christmas novella to the In the Arms of a Savage Series*)

Lovin' the Alpha of the Streets: A Valentine's Day Novella (*Valentine's Day novella to the Fallin' for the Alpha of the Streets Series*)

Awakened: A Paranormal Romance

As Long as You Stay Down

Solace in Seven

Solace II: The Final Cut
Something Bleu
Something Borrowed
Something New
The Knight Before Christmas: A Potomac Falls Short
I'll Be Home for Christmas: A Potomac Falls Short Book II
Triggered: A Potomac Falls Novella
Wasted Off You: A Friends to Lovers Novella
Because You Don't Know My Name: A Potomac Falls Novella
Will You Say My Name: A Potomac Falls Novella Book Two
Remember My Name: A Potomac Falls Novella Book Three
Every Thug Needs a Lady: A Lady and the Tramp Retelling
Ten Things I Hate About Lovin' You: An Enemies to Lovers Novella
In Exchange: An Urban Thriller
T.A.N.: An Erotic Novella

**Children's Books:**

Princess for Hire
Princess Twinkle Toes & the Missing Magic Sneakers
Little One, Change the World
Adjust Your Crown: A Self-Love Coloring Book for Children of Color

**Non-Fiction:**

Authors are a Business: The Booked & Busy Course Mini Book

# BLP

Visit bit.ly/readBLP to join our mailing list for sneak peeks and release day links!

Let's connect on social media!
Facebook - B. Love Publications
Twitter - @blovepub
Instagram - @blovepublications

**We hate errors, but we are human! If the B. Love team leaves any grammatical errors behind, do us a kindness and send them to us directly in an email to** blovepublications@gmail.com **with ERRORS as the subject line.**

**As always, if you enjoyed this book, please leave a review on Amazon/Goodreads, recommend it on social media and/or to a friend, and mark it as READ on your Goodreads profile.**

**By the Book with B Podcast: bit.ly/bythebookwithb**

www.ingramcontent.com/pod-product-compliance
Lightning Source LLC
LaVergne TN
LVHW050318160826
845677LV00014B/3466

* 9 7 9 8 9 8 8 5 8 5 1 8 3 *